UNCHARTED STORMS:

Short Stories of Hearts at Risk

by

JACKIE ANTON

RISING PHOENIX PRESS

Published by Progressive Rising Phoenix Press.
Visit www.progressiverisingphoenix.com.

Printed in the U.S.A.

ISBN-10: 1940834333
ISBN-13: 978-1-940834-33-7

1st Printing

Edited by Adele Brinkley

Cover Design by Goddess Fish

Book Layout by William Speir.
Visit www.williamspeir.com.

INTRODUCTION

Uncharted Storms:

Six young women are transported via foul weather, and perhaps fate, into bizarre circumstances.

Eleven-year-old Erica is sure the world will end in 2012, but it is eleven years later that her world is upended in the science fiction story Terra Beyond 2012.

At eighteen, Annie is working her way through college. An extended shift at the diner where she works is responsible for her being caught in near blizzard conditions. Annie is hit from behind and sent sprawling into a pile of snow. Her night only gets more terrifying from there. A Tumble in the Snow is based on a larger work, which was my November 2013 National Novel Writing Month entry, and is still in the creative process.

Chris is taking a break after completing her Associate Degree to travel the winter horse show circuit. She is on her way home with her best friend when she is injured in a traffic accident. The early spring storm, which is responsible for the devastation, catapults her and her friend on a journey back through time. Follow this pair through the storm and its aftermath in Riding Lightning.

Rounding out the collection are two slightly modified excerpts from my published works authored as J. M. Anton, which is the pseudonym used for my adult novels.

Flash Flood Texas Style is an excerpt from Fateful Waters. This adult novel was published in 2012.

Casey's weather tale involves a late night encounter in a steamy summer rain. A Rainy Night is an excerpt from the pages of Cassandra: Night Shades, which is slated for a 2015 release.

Jack counts on the torrential downpour to cloak their flight south. Wicked Winds is a bonus short story for this paperback version of "Uncharted Storms." Our hero and heroine will populate the pages of Jack's Alabama Sunrise where they are caught up in a blood feud that began with the rescue of a family member.

TABLE OF CONTENTS

TERRA BEYOND 2012

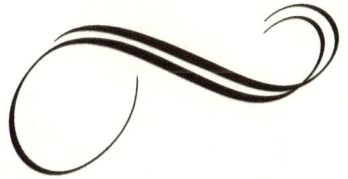

E's Eyes ONLY!

December 7, 2012

What a day! Like there isn't enough to be worried about in today's crazy world, we have to write a report on what events caused the attack on Pearl Harbor in 1941. I mean my grandmother wasn't even born yet!

I have to find a better spot to hide this journal. My brat brother has been snooping in my room again. If these pages fall into the wrong hands, like someone who will snitch to my custodial parent, I will be grounded forever.

December 8, 2012

I'm spending the weekend with Dad. Plans are for dinner out, as usual, some Christmas shopping, and a movie. Dad promised to give me a hand with my Pearl Harbor assignment.

I can't see the point in any of it! All the talk at school is about the world imploding, or ceasing to exist on December 21. At Thanksgiving, Grandma told me that during her life there had been several scares like this one. Twitter is going nuts with how the human race will go the way of the dinosaurs. Pretty scary stuff! It sure is hard to concentrate on making a Christmas list of what I want from my family when we may not see December 25th.

Just in case, I put together a short wish list.

How about: 1. Extending my eleventh birthday to April, instead of Christmas Eve?

2. Moving in with my dad?

3. Spending Christmas with Grandma, and riding her horses in the snow one more time?

2023

The ground began to convulse beneath Erica's threadbare, used, and mismatched athletic shoes. She had forgotten about the prophets of doom and gloom orbiting the planet prior to her eleventh birthday. At twenty-two, her freshly minted college degree would be of more use as butt paper.

She scanned the doorways and alleys along her route. Her goodwill outfit reflected from the occasional window. Much of the neighborhood was boarded up. A budding fashionista during her high school days, Erica had since cultivated the grunge look. The rattier the clothes the better; you could get mugged in a heartbeat if you looked like you had something worth taking.

She waved to the drab-looking clerk on her way into the store. Shelves were getting bare. She picked out a can of noodle soup and a beat-up, ancient-looking, can of tuna hiding behind a stack of spinach cans. She was moving through the aisles and scouting out the sparsely stocked shelves when they began to shake, sway, and tumble to the floor.

A loud roar filled her ears, which felt ready to pop from the increase in pressure. It reminded her of the sound of a tornado, but much louder than the few she'd been through while in college in Lubbock. The eerie sound threatened to deafen her. Black clouds formed close to the ground; her first thought was that another one of the huge oil refineries that dominated Houston had exploded. Then a blinding, blue-white, ray of light penetrated the cloud-bank. That was the last thing Erica recalled as she peeked out from under a shelf that had pinned her to the dirty, nondescript, vinyl floor of the local foodmart. Screams of terror from the street out front echoed through her mind as she lost consciousness.

Her next foray into a functional state was to open gritty, swollen, eyes to the painful glare of an overhead light. A hospital room or triage center was the first thing that registered. That thought was quickly deleted when her grandmother leaned over her.

"It's going to be all right, Little E." Grandma raised Erica's right hand and held it in hers. Grandma was one of the few people on earth who ever called her Little E.

Okay, she thought. It's time to reassess the situation. I have not been little for a long time. In a pair of heels, her five-foot-ten allowed her to look most men in the eye. Flat on her back in a strange room with her deceased grandmother leaning over her, Erica was frightened and disoriented.

"Hey! Somebody let me out of this contraption. I need a bathroom, now!" she yelled as loudly as her raspy voice and sore throat would allow her.

Not a soul responded to her urgent demands, and Granny had vanished. She began to fear the worst. The weight of the falling shelves did me in, she thought, and I'm dead. A better alternative explanation, she figured, than to admit she might have gone around the bend. Grandma had become the voice in her head who was encouraging, sympathetic to a point, Erica's taskmaster, and disciplinarian. Her grandmother's apparition had a quirky sense of humor, much as she had in life. Erica was concerned about her mental state. Her grandmother had passed from this world six years earlier.

Two silent figures entered the room. Their white uniforms fit like wetsuits; all that was visible through clear bubble-like masks were their paper-white complexions. They didn't attempt to lower the tall rails that confined her to the bed so she could relieve herself. Instead, they changed the bag floating in the air and pumping its contents into her left arm. Erica opened her mouth to protest and again to request a toilet or even a bedpan, but not a sound came from her vocal cords. One more attempt to communicate with the pair proved too much for her. Erica sank into a, cold, black void.

Erica emerged from the abyss floating among the stars. Vertigo gripped her as she gazed down at her home planet. She speculated that the scene must be what the astronauts saw when they hovered above Earth and performed the tasks of repairing the space station. Okay, so where is my spacesuit? She wondered if she was having an out-of-body experience, but didn't all the information on the subject say that people are able to see themselves when that happens? She couldn't see herself and didn't have a clue where her physical being was.

Her ride out of our solar system allowed Erica a close-up view of planets that prior to then could only be seen second hand. Out around Saturn, she briefly looked back at the fading Earth. To her dismay, the once blue planet was now a murky grayish brown. A thought penetrated her groggy consciousness; the change in color could not be a good sign.

She seemed to be picking up speed, and soon the Milky Way was far behind her. At that point, unfamiliar stars and planets whizzed past; she was aware of a tumbling sensation. Her limbs lost all feeling before a penetrating cold took hold of her. Then oblivion.

Her alien captors began the thawing process. Time had escaped Erica; she hadn't a clue how long she'd been in cryo-sleep. She possessed a smidgen of knowledge regarding cryogenics from college physics, but little was known on Earth about the effects of inducing long-term exposure to the deep freeze. Straw-like tentacles protruded from every orifice on her numb body. She was unable to open her eyes. Finally, after repeated attempts, she succeeded in focusing on her surroundings. Her heart rate doubled when her slowly clearing vision caught sight of what looked to be a huge sliver squid suspended above her. The tentacles imprisoning her traced back to the monster hovering over her strapped-down form. "Calm down, Little E. You will do yourself damage. What you see is only a medical device, which is unfamiliar to you."

I knew it! I've passed on, and this must be hell, she thought. Erica couldn't come up with another scenario to explain how she could be hearing her grandmother.

Each time she awoke, her sojourn into the strange environment lasted longer. The pale aliens who'd made first contact were conspicuously absent from her cold cell. A black robot hovered above the floor and saw to her needs. Red and blue lights flashed in a line from right to left where a human would have eyes. Its arms were similar to the automated replacements that had put millions of humans out of work. Those robots were familiar to her, but this one appeared to be a thousand times more advanced. It never spoke to her, but seemed to know Erica's every need before she could verbalize it. She wondered if it was telepathic, or was receiving instructions from beings that were. Whenever she became overly stressed, her grandmother's voice appeared out of the strange metallic odor that permeated the room.

The voice in her subconscious informed Erica that she now had an implant in her head. Its function was supposedly to enable her to speak and understand several alien languages. Her minimal biological studies were also enhanced while she slept, and while running on a round tread wheel. She felt like a hamster on that contraption, but the knowledge gained in the process helped shed some light on her captivity. She was on an incredibly advanced version of Noah's Ark!

A twenty-five year-old altered version of Erica stepped onto the surface of a new world. Truthfully, if one counted the cryo-sleep Little E was really three hundred and twenty-five. The sweet smell of wildflowers assaulted her senses and crisp clean air filled her lungs. Erica found herself surrounded by few hundred passengers; she hadn't realized there were so many others on the same journey. She speculated that the ship must have been immense if they all were kept in isolation, as she was, following their stay in the cryogenics lab. The young humans stood on a hill overlooking a lush valley. Sparkling clear water flowed over a small dam before it wandered snake-like through the breathtaking landscape.

The sky was foreign, more of a turquoise, and the clouds did appear to have a silver lining. A distant moon with a satellite of its own was clearly visible in the light of day; another, smaller, moon appeared to be setting on the horizon. The ground began to tremble, which panicked many in the group. Erica assumed they had all experienced the earthquake type trembles that she remembered before arriving on the alien transport. Erica listened to the thunder accompanying the vibrations; she felt in the soles of her leather-like boots. She recognized the cadence from her childhood. Then she saw them; hundreds of blacks, and bays, sorrels, and grays galloped with their tails flying high and manes flowing. Tears filled her eyes, and joy filled her heart at the wonder of the sight. She called to the heavens. "Look, Grandma, paradise!" Erica knew her grandmother heard her and was smiling down on her, and on the beautiful animals she'd taught Erica to appreciate.

Most of the others were younger than Erica; they appeared to be from places around Earth, or what the aliens referred to as Terra. It was her understanding that they were to be met by a representative of the indigenous population, which probably accounted for the young age of her companions. The young were more accepting of new situations, and they didn't carry the baggage or prejudices of their elders.

Erica tore her eyes from the spectacular equines quenching their thirst. She scanned the sky and the land below, but found not a sign of a transport or vehicle. A, huge, golden stallion separated from the herd to lope up the hill. Erica's companions shrieked and scattered, but she held her ground. She didn't sense any danger from the approaching horse. He was magnificent; oddly, his eyes were a deep violet. Transfixed, Erica reached out to stroke his neck when he approached her. "You're a handsome devil," she said in her native English.

Erica almost fell over from shock when he answered, "Thank you, Terran Erica. Welcome to Equus Prime."

Right before her eyes, he transformed into a huge, human-like, male; he was clad in a golden suit that hugged his impressive physique. The thin formfitting material didn't leave much to her imagination. She stood there stupefied.

He extended his hand in greeting. "I am Ambassador Quinlynn Colt from central command. I am here to escort you and the other Terrans to our capital for orientation." She continued to stare at him, but didn't acknowledge his greeting. "Terran Erica, is your translator malfunctioning?"

Erica gave herself a mental shake. "Sorry the whole shift from horse to man was a bit unexpected. So, is this your real form?"

"Would you prefer I take another?"

"Are all the horses shape-shifters?" She sounded disappointed, even to her own ears.

"Most of what you refer to as horses were transported here, much as you have been. We assume their shape to ascertain their health and learn more about them. I was led to believe you have a unique knowledge of the animals."

Erica figured that her college studies, which had been enhanced by her biology and medical training in transport, as well as her training with Grandma's horses were the reason she was chosen for relocation.

"I may have been a little premature about the paradise reference," she whispered to her grandmother. Erica had a feeling that Grandma's advice was going to prove invaluable.

She wondered what her escort's true physical form was, and where the thin device that he held in his hand had come from. He pressed the matchbox size device, which transported the group to orientation in the capital of their new home world.

A TUMBLE IN THE SNOW

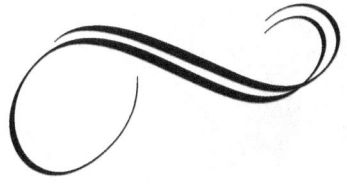

Cleveland, Ohio

Winter of 1980

Annie shrugged on her coat and was preparing to clock out when Judy came storming into the kitchen. She ripped off her apron, tossed it to the floor, looked the night manager in the eyes, and bellowed. "I quit!"

"You can't just walk out when we're so busy." Disbelief was evident in Martha's tone.

"Yeah? Watch me. One of you can kiss their butts, including that miserable creep at booth six."

Martha turned to Annie. "Can you stay for another hour of so?"

"I could, Martha, but the last bus leaves at ten thirty. How will I get home?"

"If you stay to help me out, I'll pay for a cab."

Annie agreed. She sure could use the extra money. She shucked her coat, and picked up the check pad that Judy had thrown down with her apron. Annie grabbed a clean apron, put her long blonde hair back on top of her head, scanned the orders on the clip wheel for the cooks, and looked at Judy's book of order sheets. Booth six, coffee, but no order yet.

Annie refilled the customer's mug. "May I take your order, sir?"

Mack was about ready to give her a piece of his mind when he looked up into Annie's smiling face and sparkling blue eyes. He looked around for the red head. "I'm afraid you scared her away. Won't I do?" she teased.

"You'll do just fine. How is the food in here?"

"Satisfactory," she answered in a noncommittal way.

"What the hell does that mean?" His voice had dropped from a pleasant baritone to a raspy deep bass in a heartbeat, like he was struggling to control a volatile temper. "It means I don't know your preferences. The food here isn't like Mom's home cooked meals, but it beats the heck out of pre-packaged frozen dinners.

"What's the soup of the day?" He made an effort to modulate his voice to a less hostile tone.

"Vegetable beef."

Mack ordered a bowl of soup and the double burger with fries. She smiled at him, and his long miserable day brightened a bit. She was back in a flash with his bowl of soup and a small basket of various cracker choices. He watched her make the rounds, filling orders and refilling drinks. She had an infectious smile. The little blonde waitress was polite to everyone and joked with those she knew. While he was working on his soup and tracking his substitute waitress, a gray-haired fellow sat in the booth right in front of his. Little Miss Sunshine brought Mack the burger and fries. "Here you go, enjoy!" She filled his mug, and moved to the newly occupied booth.

"Annie-O! You're here kind of late, aren't yah, kiddo?"

She filled his coffee mug. "Hey Smitty, we got real busy right around time for me to head home, and Judy quit."

"Didn't think she'd last long," he said. "No sense of humor."

"The usual, Smitty?"

"You bet, sweetie."

Smitty's usual consisted of a bowl of chili and a cheeseburger. She filled his mug when she brought his order and then moved over to refill Mack's. "Well…what do you think?" she asked, noting the dent he had put in his burger; the fries had disappeared.

"Satisfactory," he replied and grinned at her.

"Good." Was her brief reply, and then she was gone.

The late diner customers thinned out and faded into the increasing snow. Annie set a slice of pie in front of Smitty. "How are you getting home kid? The bus doesn't run this late over here."

"Martha said she would call a cab for me if I stayed to cover for Judy."

"Cabs may be hard to come by in this weather. I have to make one more stop. Second shift hadn't arrived on time, to man the loading docks, so I came over here to chow down while I wait for them to navigate the highways and arrive at work. If you can't get a cab, call dispatch and I'll pick you up on my way home.

"Thanks, Smitty."

"Annie-O!"

"What?"

"Don't you do anything dumb, like walking up to the other bus line!"

"Smitty, you worry too much. I'm a big girl."

"You do like I say, young lady."

She ignored him and moved over to Mack. "Dessert?" she inquired.

"Any suggestions?"

Smitty turned around. "Son, as far as that little lady is concerned, there's only one dessert on the menu."

"Don't harass the customers," she reprimanded him.

"So, what am I?"

"An old buttinsky," she teased, and smiled at him.

Mack liked her. It was pleasant to be around a good-natured female, for a change. He ordered a slice of apple walnut pie. Truthfully, he was stuffed and only ordered the pie to put off the decision about where he was going to sleep tonight. His apartment was only a half an hour from here, but his parents' farm was close to triple that in good weather.

"One apple walnut pie." She plunked the desert in front of him and refilled his cup once more.

"Whoa! That's one huge hunk of pie."

She brought a carryout box along with his check. "It travels well and warms up nicely in the microwave."

Smitty got to his feet, stuffed his arms into a thick waterproof jacket, and pulled his winter cap over his ears. "Got to go. Say hi to your mom, Annie-O. Give me a call if you need a ride."

"Thanks again, Smitty. Be careful driving in the snow and ice," she called after him.

Annie disappeared after her conversation with her trucker acquaintance and didn't return. Mack left a tip, paid his check, and proceeded out front to where his car sat cloaked in a thick blanket of white. He cleared a path to the door latch with his gloved hand. The Chevy sputtered to life. He cranked up the heater and defroster while he scraped and cleared the windshield. He pulled up the collar of his dad's old bomber jacket. It was really starting to blow. The streets should be quiet tonight, he thought. It wasn't a fit night for man or beast. He turned east toward town and his apartment. He was little

more than a couple of blocks down the road when he spotted a bun-
dled-up figure trudging through the drifted sidewalk. He couldn't really make out the strangely dressed pedestrian as it crossed the side
street and continued on close to the windbreak of deserted store-
fronts, but he instinctively knew it was Annie.

Cabs were backed up with a minimum two-hour wait. Annie was
beat, and she had an early morning class at Cuyahoga Community
College the next morning. She figured the busses were pretty de-
pendable, and all she had to do was walk a few blocks to catch the
one that ran all night. She stepped into her snow boots, tucked her
black work slacks into them, and pulled a Cleveland Browns sweat-
shirt over her white blouse. Layered up, she shrugged into her father's old winter coat. The wool overcoat was too large for her, but it
allowed her to pile on more clothes for warmth. It also gave her emo-
tional comfort; she felt closer to her beloved father. The coat was
only a couple of inches shy of her boot tops. She pulled her knit hat
down over her ears, and after placing her long knitted scarf around
her neck the excess was used to anchor her hat. She'd checked her
small clutch purse to make sure she had the exact change for bus fare
before converting her tips for the day into more manageable bills.
She tucked it securely into the deep right pocket of her coat, and
stepped into the storm.

Annie had taken this route countless times and it usually only
took half an hour to make the walk—ten minutes more in a heavy
rain or snow, but the wind fought her every step and nipped at any
exposed skin. She was rethinking her reluctance to call Smitty. She
reasoned that it was as far to return as to go on, so she struggled
through the drifts on the sidewalk. The snowplows had made a pass,
a while back and added to the depth of the drifts when crossing the
streets. She was wishing she had a few more layers beneath her nearly
snow-covered coat when she noticed a car pull up ahead of her and
stop. Annie was fairly street smart. She stopped and began to cross to
the opposite side of the street so she wouldn't be trapped between
the car and the buildings if the occupants were up to no good.

Mack saw her make a move to cross the icy street. He attempted to roll down the window to call out to her, but the damn thing
was iced shut. He opened the door to get out and identify himself
when he saw a pair of high beam headlights swing around the corner.
The idiot driver began to slide all over the road, and Annie was right
in middle of the oncoming car's path.

Annie caught sight of the speeding car about the same time that
Mack had. The vehicle was sliding all over, and she didn't know
which way to move to avoid being mowed down. She never had a
chance to move at all. She was hit from behind. The impact lifted her
off of her feet, and she lost her breath upon her return to earth.
Thankfully, a snowplow drift cushioned her landing.

Mack rolled her over and brushed the snow from her face.
"Annie, are you all right?"

"What happened?" She croaked, her voice little more than a
whisper.

"Other than attempting to get yourself killed? Not much." He
spoke to her with a disgusted parental tone that gave her pause.

Who the heck was he to reprimand her? Annie tried to sit up,
but she was still gasping for air. "Did the car hit me?"

"No."

Oh, that really clears things up, she thought. "Well...something
did." She was struggling to focus.

"I did."

She waited for him to elaborate. Finally, she asked. "You did?"

"I just told you that," he said in exasperation as he helped her
to stand. She seemed shaky and disoriented. He gripped her upper
arm to steady her. "Come on, Annie, let's go."

"Where?" She resisted his hold on her.

"Out of this shit!" he snarled.

Annie caught sight of the car that she had been avoiding before
she went airborne. She spun around to shove him with both hands
placed on his chest. Mack lost his footing and landed on his seat in
the icy street. Then she hightailed it down the sidewalk as fast as the
treacherous footing would allow.

Mack couldn't believe the little brat had caught him off guard.
He'd most likely saved her life, and what did she do to express her
gratitude? She'd flattened him! He should let her fend for herself; in-

stead, he went after her. He caught up and swung her around by the arm to face him. At that point, she tried to plant a facer on him, but he caught her hand and pinned it to her side. She attempted to kick him, and they both went down again. Once more, he stood and offered her his hand; she tried to kick his legs out from under him. "That's the last straw!" he growled in to the biting wind.

None too gently, he yanked her to a standing position, removed her scarf, and tied it around her. Even with her hands pinned to her side she continued to squirm and kick. He lifted her up over his left shoulder, like a sack of potatoes. She kicked and cussed him up one side and down the other. Mack brought his right hand down on her rear end. She kicked and screamed foul epitaphs above the screech of the rising storm. He gave her a couple of more good swats before depositing his captive onto the front seat of his car. Keeping a close eye on Annie, he went around the front of the vehicle and slid behind the steering wheel. It was obvious that he had frightened her. "How old are you, Annie?"

"Why?"

Mack made a superhuman effort to control his irritation. He tried to project a calm demeanor and voice inflection. "Can't you just answer a simple question?"

Annie was terrified, but she didn't want him to know it. "Eighteen." Her voice sounded kind of feeble.

"You sure don't look like you're that old." She didn't say a word, but continued to stare at him with the biggest blue eyes he had ever seen. "You act more like you're ten," he commented obviously disgusted with her.

"That would make you a child molester, then. Wouldn't it?"

"Annie, I'm not going to molest you." He tried for calm and reasonable again.

"So, what are you going to do?"

"Drive you home."

She was assessing him as if he were mentally impaired. "You can't take me home."

"Why not?"

"Because, you don't know where I live."

"Granted. Suppose you clear that up and tell me?"

Her voice turned belligerent. "No."

He was genuinely perplexed. "Why?"

"I don't want you to know where I live, that's why."

"Look, Annie, I'm tired and running out of patience. Now, where do you live?"

"Go to hell!" She tried to shout out the direction she wished him to take.

Mack was at the end of his rope. He figured she must have some identification on her. He reached for the front of her coat to check her pockets. When he reached for her she kicked him. "Damn little brat!" He captured her legs to place them on either side of his body, and hauled her into his lap. That effectively nullified her ability to kick him. Annie wriggled all the more and tried to fight him. Her gyrations were arousing a long denied need in him, which was the last thing he wanted at that moment. She would think for sure he was intent on raping her. He thought she might have a wallet in her slack pockets, so he worked up her ridiculously long coat to check it out. He was mentally frisking her as impersonally as he did in his day-to-day handling of those arrested for various offenses. He slid his hands back to where her back pockets should be, and she made another attempt at freedom. Exhausted and angry, Mack forced her back into his lap—big mistake!

Annie was becoming frightened beyond reason. She was tied; her hands were of no use and becoming numb. He had taken away the use of her legs. Now he was trying to get into her pants! Her eyes filled with tears. She could feel his arousal pushing against her through their clothing. "No! Please, she begged. Terrified, she froze and went perfectly still. "Please don't hurt me. Just let me go."

Mack knew exactly what was going through her mind. "Annie," he said softly. "I'm not going to rape you, so calm down."

"You're not?" she whispered as she fought to control her fear.

"Annie, I'm only trying to find some identification that will give me a clue where you live." She stared at him, but didn't utter a word. It was obvious she had trust issues. "Don't you carry a purse, or a wallet?"

"Yes, it's in my coat pocket." She came close to blurting out that it wasn't in her pants pockets, but thought better of it.

"No, I checked your coat first. The pockets are empty."

"I must have dropped it when the car didn't hit me."

He didn't miss the sarcasm regarding his rescue. "Stay put!" he warned her as he pocketed the keys, opened the car door, and trudged back into the storm.

Once the car door closed behind him, Annie began working to free her hands. He'd tied her scarf securely with the knot at her back, and she was having a devil of a time trying to loosen it. Exhausted, she gave up the attempt.

Searching in the snow had helped Mack to cool his rising temper and get his body under control. It was obvious, to him, that he had frightened Annie with his physical reaction to their struggle. You sure haven't handled this situation very well, he thought, and made a conscious effort to alleviate the tension. "I found it!" He smiled at her as he entered the relatively warm confines of the Chevy.

He started the engine once more and cranked up the heater before turning to address his passenger "Okay, Annie, are you going to cooperate and tell me where you live, or do I have to go through your purse?" She stared at him like a kid caught with her hand in the cookie jar. She was scrunched up against the passenger door with her with her knees bent to her chest and her feet planted on the seat between them. "Turn around, Annie, and put your feet on the floor" he ordered as he flipped on the dim overhead light to find a final destination for this botched rescue attempt.

"I can't," she sniffled and squelched the threatening tears.

"Why not?" This kid was driving him to distraction.

"Because, I'm stuck." Annie nodded her head for emphasis, and the dreaded tears escaped to roll down her cheeks.

He cautiously instructed her to stretch her legs out behind his back, so he could untie her. "Annie, you kick me again, and I'm going to give you the spanking of your life. Do you understand?" She only nodded. He moved closer to loosen the knot. Great! She had tried to work the scarf loose using the window crank to pry the knot apart. It was jammed up tight between the crank and the door. She was indeed stuck, and he couldn't budge it. He reached into the glove compartment to pull out an old leather scabbard and removed a hunting knife.

Annie took one look at the knife in his hand and panicked. "NO!"

"Annie, I'm not going to hurt you. This is only to cut you free."

"No. Please, don't cut it!" She was bawling in earnest now.

He wondered how his psychology professors would handle this situation. He asked for clarification. "Now, what?"

"My grandmother made it for me," she choked out between sobs.

"Well, have her make you another one" he replied in a reasonable tone.

"She's dead."

The sadness of her voice and the tears cascading down her face moved Mack to depths of his, fast-growing cynical, heart. "Shit!" He reached behind her, latched on to the crank with both hands, and pulled it out of the door. The sudden release propelled Annie against his chest. Mack pulled away from her like he'd been scalded. "There, now, are you happy?" He threw the sheathed knife under the seat as he repositioned his unruly body behind the steering wheel.

"I'm sorry you had to break the door, but you scared me, and I tried to escape."

"You should be afraid." He continued to scold her while driving through the hazardous conditions toward the lower west side of town.

"Well…this whole incident is your fault!" She nodded her head for emphasis and glared at him.

"My fault? How the do you figure that?" He could feel her blue eyes boring holes through him, but he focused on the road.

"If it wasn't for your sunny disposition and winning personality, Judy wouldn't have quit, and I could have caught my usual bus home."

Mack couldn't believe her reasoning. "Okay, it's my fault, and I'll see you home safely."

The side roads were in worse shape than the main streets. He concentrated on driving; neither of them uttered another word after her statement placing the blame on his back. He tried to remember the old saying about "no good deed going unpunished." He scanned their surroundings as they approached her address. "Jesus, Annie, you come home alone at this time of night and walk these streets?" He hadn't done a very good job of hiding his disapproval.

"How else am I supposed to get home from the bus stop? Fly?"

"Don't get sassy with me, young lady!"

"Then don't ask stupid questions."

He'd parked where she indicated and turned off the ignition. He opened the door and was about to walk around to assist her through the drifts when she demanded to know what he thought he was doing. "I'm escorting to your door," he replied in a tone that defied her to argue. He guided her to the side entrance of an old paint chipped duplex that had a front porch on both levels. They trudged through drifts to a side entrance and then proceeded to the upper level where a small landing separated a front and rear unit. He'd noticed a similar layout on the first floor when they entered. Four apartments were housed within what looked like any other duplex on the street.

Annie stopped on the landing outside her door and turned to face him. "Thank you for the ride."

He would probably never know what had possessed him; perhaps there'd been a devil on his shoulder. He stared into her blue eyes. "Have you ever been kissed by a man, little Annie?" Mack pocketed his gloves to take her face between his hands. He brushed his thumb over her lower lip as he asked the question. She trembled at his touch, but he was experienced enough to know her response wasn't fear.

"Of course," she whispered in a shaky voice.

He moved closer so their bodies touched, and she backed into her door.

She began to tremble as he followed her retreat toward the door, and she could feel his body heat through her layers of cold weather protection. "Really?" He challenged in a deep sensual voice that sent shivers through her. She only nodded, like a goofy bobble-head version of herself. She began to wonder seriously about her sanity. She'd been trying to escape from him a short time earlier; now, she wanted to wrap herself around him.

His kiss was soft and tentative, but her lips instinctively parted. He deepened the kiss, and she lost all self-control. She threw her arms around his neck and responded like a harlot! The thickness of their coats seemed like a six-foot-wide wall between them. She was experiencing a need to be closer.

He rasped her name in what was close to a painful plea. "Annie, I need you."

The depth of feeling in his voice so moved her that she was ready to give herself to him right there on the lading, but Mac saved her virtue. He'd been standing on the other side of the door listening and waiting for his beloved mistress. He grew impatient and began to bark. Mack released her and stood there shaking as if he were a kid going through puberty who had just been confronted by a gun-toting father.

"Quiet! Mac, it's okay, it's only me." She kept her voice low, but he obeyed the command.

Her rescuer began to laugh. "Your dog's name is Mack?"

She gazed into his smiling face. "Yes. What's so funny about that?"

He shook his head and backed away from her. "Not a thing sweetheart. You better go in." He started down the stairs.

"Wait!"

He turned back toward her and raised his right eyebrow in question. She walked to the top step. "I don't know your name."

He took her face in his hands and planted a fatherly kiss on her forehead. "It doesn't matter, does it?"

She reached out and touched the ring on his left hand. "I guess it doesn't." Tears began to trickle down her face. Annie watched him remove his black leather gloves from the pocket of his jacket. He pulled them on while descending to the first floor. Once more, the offending gold band was obscured from her view. She wiped her eyes with her scarf as she continued to watch him walk into the snowy night and out of her life.

Fate sure was a miserable tease, she thought as she pondered the unlikely prospect of ever meeting him again.

The End, or The Beginning?

RIDING LIGHTNING

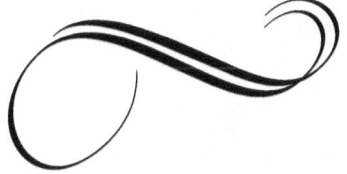

Chapter One

A lightning flash followed by the earsplitting sound of an exploding electrical transformer jolted Chris from her slumber. Now, bolt upright in the passenger bucket seat of the one-ton Ram crew cab, she turned toward the driver. "Where are we?"

"Damned if I know," her gray-haired boss growled in frustration. "I can't see a worth spit in this deluge. We may have missed our turn off. The GPS is worthless, and all I can get is static on the CB."

Chris gave her iPhone a try. "No cell reception either! Can't we stop until the storm eases up?"

"Don't you think I would if I could find a spot to pull this rig off the road?" He had to shout to be heard over the thunderstorm and the CB static. "See if you can raise someone on that thing. Could be there is a place close by that we can put up for a while."

Chris unbuckled her seat belt to reach the unit, which was positioned closer to the driver's side, and was occupied checking the bands most used by truckers when she heard Mr. Russell curse. She glanced up, but could barely discern the red hood of the pickup, let alone the road in front of it. Then a flash of lightning revealed a semi coming toward them. It was straddling the centerline, or where she estimated it should be. The driver of the oncoming eighteen-wheeler corrected his path at the last moment to avoid a head on collision.

The monstrous vehicle missed the cab, but ripped the side of horse trailer open. Above the sounds of the storm, crashing metal, and shattering glass, she heard the screams of the three horses they were hauling. Then she was tumbling through the air. Chris felt an excruciating pain knife through her head as she impacted with a rocky surface.

It was difficult to determine the passage of time as she dialed back into reality. Pain was playing around the edges of her slowly functioning mind. How long had she lain in the rain? The fog was lifting from her mental process, but the downpour obstructed her vision. Still groggy, she attempted a sitting position only to fall onto her back. She made a valiant effort to call out to her companions, but nearly choked on the persistent rain. She slowly rolled onto her side and called out again, but her vocal cords refused to co-operate.

Chris couldn't hear a thing other than the raging storm. Thunder echoed in her throbbing head. She felt warm breath on her face and in her ear. Someone was checking her out, but she couldn't hear a voice.

Frustrated with her lack of response, he nudged her back. She groaned, so he stepped back and waited for her to acknowledge him. She rolled onto her back once more. Still, Chris had failed to speak to him; he nudged her shoulder a bit harder. She screamed in pain, and her eyes flew open. She had startled him. Backing away, he kept a watchful eye on her.

Chris was challenged to focus on the immediate area; it was very dark. She wondered if night was falling or it was the total lack of sunlight. Someone was out there, but she was unable to see. She figured since she was able to shriek like a banshee, she could try calling out once more. "Who's there?" No reply. "Mr. Russell? Karen?"

Hesitant footsteps crunched over the rock-strewn ground; a twig snapped under his weight. Chris's nerves were raw. She could feel his presence, but he kept silent. Suddenly, lightning lit up the darkness to reveal his huge form standing over her; another flash allowed her to see his big brown eyes as he kept his vigil. Her left arm was closest to him, but it hurt like hell and was essentially useless. She spoke to him in a calm voice. "Was that bump to my left shoulder really necessary?" She reached out with her right hand, slowly, so she wouldn't startle him again.

He responded to her outstretched hand. When Chris made the connection he pulled her to her feet. The pain as he hauled her to a standing position threatened to return her to the void she had so recently escaped. She wrapped her good arm around his neck and leaned against his muscular chest; the move kept her from falling flat on her face. She feared losing consciousness, figuring that if she did she would never wake up. He stood, patiently, waiting to see what she would require of him.

"Well, handsome, let's see if you and I can locate the others."
Each step was torture, but the fear of the others being in worse shape
drove her on. She picked her way toward where she thought the road
should be located. Flashlights and headlights lit the mangled remains
of their rig.

When they'd started the short, but painful walk back toward the
scene of the wreck he'd walked with her and allowed her to use his
body to support herself. Chris felt him hesitate. The odor of burnt
tires, spilled diesel, and blood caused them both momentarily to lose
sight of their purpose. They had resumed the small climb back up to
the highway when a huge sphere of lightning struck, sending a charge
through them both.

The storm had eased to a light rain as dawn broke. Boomer
scanned the immediate area. He was hungry and thirsty, but he didn't
want to leave Chris. She was sprawled at his feet, quiet and unmov-
ing, but he sensed that she was alive. He was still standing guard
when she finally opened her eyes. They heard voices. He waited to
see if she would call out, but when she didn't he remained silent. He
was more focused on the dog-like creatures skulking in the trees below them.

Chris listened to the unfamiliar dialect as the voices drew near-
er. She couldn't find the strength to call for help, and prayed Boomer
would do something to attract their attention.

"Don´ think those folks are from these parts, Billy Jo." The
voice sounded young, to Chris—perhaps a teenage boy.

"Na, Travis. 'Taint seen ´em ´afore." The second person
sounded much younger, and Chris was having trouble following his
speech pattern. Then, the voices became eerily quiet.

Travis winced as he passed by the broken remains of the man
and woman in the road; the horses were ripped open, and it appeared
wolves had been at all of them. Their belongings were strewn over
the road and the side of the mountain below it.

"Ana´ thin´ good?" Billy Jo inquired as he spotted some inter-
esting debris further off the road.

"Not much. Some blankets, pots, an´ a stick or two of furniture
that ain't busted. The rest is kindlin´….Billy Jo, hold up. Don't go off
on your own."

Furniture? What furniture? Chris couldn't figure out that comment, unless the truck that hit them had been a moving van. Her memory was vague about the rain-shrouded truck. The last clear memory she had, before dozing off, was the detour on I-40. Traffic had been rerouted, and she never got the chance to ask Mr. Russell if they had made it to I-75 before the accident. She listened to the boys argue as they drew closer.

Billy Jo ignored his brother's warning. "Trav! Somfins' stirin' down yonder." Chris could hear the mud and rocks moving as the boy hurried toward them. She feared they would all be buried beneath a rockslide. Boomer snorted at the careless boy. Travis was in hot pursuit of his reckless little brother. He skidded to a stop, raised his rifle, then lowered it, and stood as transfixed as his brother.

Before them stood a beautiful blood bay stallion. Large blotches of mud covered his hide, but where the rain had washed it away his coat glistened in the morning sunlight. He stood his ground while he assessed the threat level of the new arrivals. Travis was doing much the same. He had seen plenty of horses; they were prevalent on the farms and plantations before the war, but he'd never encountered one like this. The horse was unusually marked: no leg markings, a star dead center of his forehead, and his eyes were ringed with white. The white around his eyes would have been enough to unnerve most grown men. It was common knowledge when you could see the white of a horse's eyes, you had trouble. They were either terrified or mean as hell, but this one only stood watching them. Travis heard a soft groan. The horse responded by lowering his head to inspect the limp form in front of his mud-covered hooves. A hand reached out to stroke his muzzle; he nickered softly, and then looked at the boys again.

Boomer backed away as the boys approached Chris, but he watched them closely for any sign of trickery. The older boy bent down and leaned over Chris.

The person on the ground was small—not much larger than Billy Jo—and covered in mud. It was obvious to Travis, based on the trousers, short hair, and strange-looking puffy vest, the injured person was a young male of indeterminate age. "Can you move?"

"No," came the hoarse reply. "The others?"

"All dead," he replied to the frantic question, as if it was an everyday occurrence to run across dead bodies scattered on the road.

"I think lightning hit me last night, and I can't seem to move. My arm hurts, and my head feels like it is going to explode."

Travis sent Billy Jo home on the old mule, they'd ridden to the scene of the wreck, to fetch their mother. "Go get Maw and the wagon. Looks like he's hurt pretty bad."

"Boomer?"

Travis was trying to figure out the strange question. Then the horse stepped forward a few steps. Maybe that was the horse's name. Travis was afraid to move the injured person, and he didn't know how to render aid, so he sat next to the prone figure and talked. "Is Boomer the stallion's name?"

"Is he injured?" Boomer was supporting her when she felt the charge flow through her.

"A few scrapes, bout all. The horse belong to you?" No answer. Travis examined the stranger's face. The eyes were closed, and he was barely breathing. He wondered, for the first time, whether he should have sent his brother to fetch their mother; the stranger would probably be dead before they could come with the wagon. He scrutinized the strange markings on the horse that stood watching his every move. For the first time, he noticed the white frosting on his hips. "You're a strange lookin´ nag! Put together nice, ´cept for those danged scary white-rimmed eyes. Could still be able to get a good price for you, if your friend goes on to meet the maker."

Chris awoke in a strange bed, totally disoriented and only vaguely able to recall the accident. Everything else was a jumble of nightmares and hallucinations. She scanned the dimly lit, sparsely decorated, room. Considering her battered condition, splitting headache, and the pain shooting through her left arm, a hospital was the most likely scenario.

On her next waking, Chris deleted any thought of having made it to a hospital or clinic. Well, I'm not dead she thought. She didn't figure dead people felt the immense pain that wracked her entire body. She'd heard there were places in the Smokey Mountains where time seemed to have stood still, but this room was extremely backwoods and didn't bode well for her level of care. To top everything off, she didn't recall where her identification and medical cards were.

Probably in her handbag, which had been in the cab of the pickup last she could recall seeing it.

"Good morning!" a cheerful voice greeted Chris. Its owner tied back the thick drapes.

Chris squinted at the sudden intrusion of sunlight. "Good morning." Her voice sounded as painful and raspy as it felt.

The woman halted midway across the room and looked at her askance before hustling to close the door. Her bright warm smile had turned into a worried frown as she approached the bed; she seated her large frame on the side of the bed and patted Chris's hand. Then she proceeded to place her other hand on Chris's forehead. "Fever is gone."

Her nurse was comforting, and Chris hoped she would answer some of her most urgent questions. "Where am I?"

"You don't know?'

"No. I can't remember much after the accident."

Her mocha complexion deepened as a frown increased the worried expression in her dark eyes. "Folks here bouts call me Hester. You remember your name?"

"Chris." Her name came out weak, barely above a whisper.

"Child, tell me you ain't a Yankee!"

"Does it matter?"

"The folks in this here house don't take kindly to Yankees. They'd like as not throw you back down the mountain."

Chris filed away Hester's reference to a house, not a hospital or clinic. "Terrific! Just what I need at the moment — people who don't know that stupid war ended a long time ago." Chris sighed deeply and closed her eyes against the pain behind them.

"Tell me, Little Miss Yankee, who won our stupid war?"

Chris's eyes popped open to the sight of a tall, lean, blonde woman standing in the doorway. She was austere. Her hair was tied back in a tight bun, and her high necked long cotton dress was covered by an off-white bib apron. The forty-something newcomer appeared to have stepped out of another century. Chris wondered if the person who was standing at the foot of the bed, peering at her with the intense blue eyes, also wore bloomers.

"I take it you aren't willing to share the outcome with us?"

Oh boy, she thought, how do I answer that? "I'm sorry," she choked out. "What did you ask?"

"Who won?" Her voice turned more hostile.

"No one." Chris felt that imparting the outcome to this woman was not in her best interest.

The newcomer stood glaring down at Chris. Then the frightening woman crossed her arms and struck a more menacing pose. "You telling me the war comes down to a draw?"

"No, I only meant no one ever wins in something so destructive."

"Hester, fix our guest some broth."

Chris noticed the subservient way Hester curtseyed to the other woman. "Yes 'um."

"And Hester, not a word about our guest being a Yankee."

Hester nodded. She gave Chris an encouraging smile before retreating and closing the door behind her. Chris felt like Dorothy in the presence of the Wicked Witch of the West.

"Do you feel up to some conversation?"

More like some interrogation Chris thought, but maybe her interrogator could also supply some information. "I suppose so. How long have I been here?"

"You've been flat on your back since Travis, Billy Jo, and I carted you home four days ago."

"The others?"

"We buried what the wolves left." Tears rolling down Chris's face onto the pillow that cradled her head prompted the next inquiry. "Were those folks your kin?"

Chris struggled to control her voice. "No. I worked for them. They were good friends,"

The older woman eyed the frail girl skeptically. Perhaps she was an indentured servant. "Where were y'all going?"

Chris struggled to rid her mind of her grief and control the increasing pain within her body. Thinking and talking were fast eluding her, but she attempted to answer. "Home."

"Where were you coming from?"

Chris made one last attempt to comply with her inquisitor "Raleigh, North Caro...." Her voice faded as she lost consciousness.

Hester tended Chris. She fed her, bathed her, saw to the changing of her bedclothes, and even helped her relieve herself. Chris found the whole process extremely embarrassing, but Hester seemed to enjoy her assigned tasks and brief conversations with her patient.

Hester's hefty, big-bosomed, form and sunny disposition were an immense comfort to Chris. Her nurse was the one constant as she drifted between murky oblivion and moments of clarity.

She had more lengthy visits with Hester, and vaguely recalled return visits from the scary blonde woman. Her surroundings continued to confuse her, but her nurse dismissed her disorientation as the effects of the laudanum that the sawbones who'd set her arm had prescribed. Hester's reference to the doctor as a sawbones didn't do a lot to relieve her patient's mind.

Somewhere between worlds Chris began to have horrendous nightmares. Whenever she was alone during her wakeful periods, she would try to piece together what had happened.

Chapter Two

To the best of her recollection, she, Mr. Russell, and his daughter, Karen, had started for home following a successful outing at the Carolina Classic. Everyone was able to unwind, and all were in good spirits.

Bill Jacobs owned the farm where Bud Russell and Chris worked. It was Mr. Jacob's habit to fly his family in to compete at many of the shows on the winter circuit and the major early spring competitions.

Bill Jacobs said his farewell to his trainer. "We'll see you in a few days Bud." The two men shook hands, and then Bill, his wife and their two grandchildren hurried off in the rented Durango to catch their flight home.

Mr. Russell's suggestion for dinner out was met with great enthusiasm. They'd been on the road since mid-February, and it was now well into May. Seldom were they able to have a relaxed meal at a sit-down restaurant; it would be a real treat. Chris was looking forward to a relaxed evening and a good night's sleep after she finished bedding down the horses, but a late evening thunderstorm put an end to her rest. Tee Jay was acting up and they were worried about possible colic, so she spent the night on a cot in front of his stall.

Early the following morning, they fed and watered the horses. Tack trunks and saddles were loaded while the horses chowed down breakfast. Two of the horses were already in the trailer, and they were in process of loading Boomer when Karen returned from the truck. She'd been sitting in the back seat of the crew cab, her preferred spot, and texting her friends about her estimated time of arrival when her dad's phone distracted her. She was waving his cell phone. "Dad! Dad! Mr. Jacobs wants to talk to you."

Chris let Boomer munch some grass while Mr. Russell took his phone call. She remembered overhearing part of the conversation.

"Hey, Bill, how was your flight? I don't know about doing that on this trip. It would be better if I came back for the mare after we get the others back home. We're all pretty road weary, and the horses could use a rest. Tee Jay was reluctant to load up this morning, and that isn't at all like him. Yeah. Okay, we'll stay put until hearing back from you." He stuffed the annoying contraption into a back pocket of his Wranglers, then he turned to Chris. "Put Boomer back in his stall and give the others some hay."

"What's up?" Chris inquired when the horses all had hay.

"Bill wants us to make a side trip to pick up a mare he bought."

"Where is she?"

"Somewhere on the western end of the state."

"Wouldn't it make more sense to go home, and then come back for her with the smaller trailer?"

He just shrugged. "What makes sense to you and me doesn't matter much."

"Sorry, girls, but it looks like we won't get home for another day or two. Karen put the farm address into the GPS, and we'll double check it with the road atlas as soon as we load Boomer."

Chris vaguely remembered checking the road map for an alternate route when they hit the detour. She thought they'd made it back onto I-40 shortly before their planned exit near a town called Statesville. She didn't recall arriving to pick up the new horse.

Chris was saved from the frustrating jumble of memories that she couldn't quite piece together by Hester's voice. "You want to sit in the chair while I tidy up? After lunch, we'll see if you can walk around the room."

Chris smiled at her. "That sounds like a plan!" Hester wore a puzzled expression, and Chris guessed that once more her speech had confounded the other woman.

Her first walkabout almost ended in disaster. She caught her reflection in a large, oak-framed, free-standing mirror that was placed next to an antique wardrobe cabinet. She would have keeled over had not Hester been supporting her. The mirrored image looked worse than she felt at that point in time. Her face was pasty, and her hazel eyes were encased in a raccoon-like mask. Her short stylish cut had grown ragged, and her auburn locks were singed. The hair on her head stood on end, like she'd stuck her hand on one of those crazy spheres at the science center. To make matters worse, she had a jagged, hairless, scar parting the unholy mess above her right eye.

Travis came to visit Chris after she found out that Boomer had, indeed, made the trip with her. It was like pulling teeth to get him to impart any information on the stallion's condition. The same old line that Boomer was doing about as well as could be expected was wearing thin with her. After a week of evasion, she feared the worst.

Travis wasn't much of a liar, and Chris figured that he'd been ordered not to upset her. She also realized that she was most likely a frightening sight, but his refusal to look her in the eye was not in character for the confident blue-eyed teen. His dark brown hair fell in waves to the color of his gray, homespun shirt, which was in jeopardy of splitting at the seams. He was beginning to develop a body that would put many fitness nuts to shame.

Chris had begun to walk several times during the day. A week after her first walkabout, she was pacing the room, and she'd started an exercise routine whenever she was alone. She found her own clothes in the wardrobe on one of her exploratory walks. Her hair was still unruly, but the bald spot had begun to grow some hair. The ragged scar was being covered by white hair.

She was dressed in her patched Wranglers, stitched up blue plaid shirt, and navy vest. Chris was sure that the repair work on the, flannel snap-front, shirt and her, fiber-filled, nylon vest had been Hester's handiwork. I wonder what she thought of the strange materials she pondered while pulling on her rough-out western boots. She was prepared to confront Travis and convince him to take her to see Boomer.

Chris climbed out the bedroom window behind Travis. She knew as soon as he helped her to the ground and before their arrival at an old bank barn that she wasn't as fit as she thought. It seemed like five miles to her, but in reality it was only a couple of hundred feet downhill, from the house. Chris bent over gasping for breath. She needed a few moments to recover before entering the barn.

Boomer was stalled in a crude, dark, stall at the rear of the lower level. He nickered to her as she entered. Exhausted, she leaned on

Travis as she hobbled past an old chestnut mare and a large mule that looked at her with his huge ears at full alert. Chris stroked the stallion's neck while assessing his condition. She ran her fingers over a three-cornered scar on his right shoulder. She turned to Travis with fire blazing in her eyes. "Is this what you call a few scrapes and bruises?"

"That was the deepest wound, and I had to stitch it. It healed well, and I removed the stitches a few days ago. Strange that his legs only had a few scrapes while the rest of him looked like he'd been through the fires of hell." Following that unsettling comment, he opened the stall gate, which creaked on a pair of forged iron hinges. "There wasn't much that I could do for the burn on his left shoulder though. I just smeared a salve that Hester gave me over it."

Chris was horrified. Boomer had a jagged scar nearly six inches long on his shoulder where he'd been supporting her when they were hit with a bolt from the stormy sky. She didn't know what to say, and her eyes were leaking rivers again. She cleared her throat. "Where is his halter, Travis?" she inquired as she mopped up the trail of tears with the sleeve of her shirt.

"He didn't have one on when we found him." Travis tried to lighten up the situation. "Ya ought to change his name to Lightning, what with the white hair growing in over the burn," he joked, and let loose with a nervous laugh.

Chris figured that Boomer's halter had broken during the wreck when he, like her, was catapulted off the side of the road. "What about his shipping boots?"

"His what?"

"Were his legs wrapped when you found us?"

Travis only shook his head in the negative. He avoided additional questions by pitching some hay to each of his charges. The more Travis talked with this Yankee female, the more confused he got. He'd begun to wonder where she had come from; he didn't think that the folks up north were all that much more advanced than they were. "We better head back up to the house before Hester finds out you're gone. Maw will skin me if she finds out about this."

Her climb back up the hill to the house was even longer than the trip to the barn had been. Travis picked her up and shoved her back through the window where she plopped onto the floor like a dead fish. He helped her off with her vest and boots while she sat on in the chair where he'd deposited her. He kept an eye on her while he stashed her clothes in the wardrobe. She fell asleep in the chair. Travis lowered the window and then exited the room by way of the door, like today had only been a regular visit.

Chris slept through dinner and was roused by Hester the following morning for her breakfast, which was followed by her normal post-meal routine. She felt like a limp rag doll when she first woke, but her mind was functioning well enough to realize she was back in a cotton nightdress; she wonder where the heck her clothes had gone. She also prayed it was Hester who had removed her clothes.

A few days later, she made her second trip to the barn accompanied by Travis, his mother, and Hester. Her escort stayed intact for the better part of a week while she grew stronger and was able to climb the hill to the house without assistance.

Boomer hadn't been out of his stall in the dark recesses of the windowless bank barn since their arrival in this alternate reality, or time warp. Chris wasn't sure how to characterize their current circumstances. The young horse refused to budge from his stall when Travis tried to lead him out for some exercise. She thanked the heavens that her equine friend's stall was large enough for him to move around freely. She was able to coax him to follow her out into a large corral where his two equine neighbors and a couple of dairy cows were turned out. Boomer paid them no mind and stuck close to her.

The following week Chris tried to free lunge him using only her voice, body language, and signaling with her functional right hand. Her audience was entranced with her ability to communicate with the horse. He continued to work in a large circle around Chris. An occasional buck erupted, but he picked up every cue. Another week and he was moving more freely and playing a bit as he went through his paces.

Their audience grew as word spread about the lightning horse. Billy Jo was joined by some of Hester's children the afternoon that Chris climbed onto Boomer's back. She coaxed him over to the fence after their normal workout routine, grabbed a fistful of mane, and swung up on the offside.

Boomer stood quietly waiting for her to ask something of him. Chris started off walking, and then asked him for a jog trot that shot arrows of pain through her left arm. A few laps was about all she could manage, and her legs felt like rubber when she again slid to the ground on the usual left side—in deference to her injured left arm.

As the days passed, the two storm refugees grew stronger. Chris' offer to help with household or barn chores was summarily dismissed, so she spent more time grooming and working with Boomer. Their workouts got longer, and Travis offered to have Hester's husband, Harvey, make a pair of shoes for him. Chris politely declined the kind offer. She was sure the only reason that Boomer had survived was that he'd stepped off a shoe, on the last slide, at the Classic Show, and her boss had decided to pull the rest of his shoes. Boomer was on his way home to stand at stud to a few select mares and would have had his shoes removed before any courting began.

Chris and Boomer were firing on all cylinders a short two weeks later when a couple of strangers showed up with the group of usual onlookers. Travis, Hester, and even Billy Jo had collected strips of cloth that Chris was able to weave into a cloth halter with a set of attached reins. It appeared that Billy Jo had forgiven Chris for turning out to be a girl, and the blue-eyed freckle faced redhead would occasionally speak to her.

Chris and Boomer were in a private place as they practiced a few maneuvers. She loped him around a while changing leads on the fly. They executed a few run downs with soft stops and rollbacks. Boomer was warmed up and raring to go. He picked up speed on a rundown, and then stuck his tail in the dirt. Barefoot, he slid a good ten feet, and his back up was explosive. Chris sat deep and asked him for an easy spin each direction. The spins were a bit faster than she'd hoped for, but she knew what he was capable of, and he had taken care of her by holding back. He stood quietly while she caught her breath. It was then that she noticed the strangers. One of the men had an ancient, box-like, camera mounted on a large wooden tripod. Billy Jo was bending the photographer's companion's ear, and the man was busy scribbling on a notepad.

Travis wasn't happy with the news of Chris and Boomer being spread around. She'd confided in him, when he offered one of his bridles for her use, that she'd begun to suspect the lightning strike had somehow moved them back through time. "I don't want anything metal on him should it strike twice, and we get a chance to go home." At first he'd thought that the bump on her head accounted for some of her strange ideas, but now he wasn't sure. Was she lost in time as she claimed?

Chris bolted upright from a sound sleep. Another loud explosion that shook her bed and rattled the windows explained the frightening wakeup call. She would never again complain about the ringing of the house phone when they were lucky enough to stay at a motel that offered wakeup service.

Hester added to her stress by placing her breakfast on the chair next to her bed, and literally throwing her clothes at her. "Hurry, child, get dressed and eat quickly. Travis is packing up already."

She didn't dawdle, but Travis was mounted on the mule and holding Boomer by his handmade halter reins. Billy Jo was on the old chestnut, and he didn't look at all happy.

The horses danced as another explosion vibrated beneath their hooves. The boy's mother kissed then both. "Now, hurry! Go high up the mountain, keep out of sight, and stay away from the roads,"

Travis didn't want to leave his mother, but she convinced him of the necessity. "Harvey and the children have taken the cows up to the caves behind the house. Hester and I will carry up some food and a few other supplies. There is not room for the horses and old Jack. They will be killed and eaten, or stolen if they remain here. Go!" Another explosion punctuated her final command.

The mounted trio picked their way up the steep slope weaving between the thickening pines and hardwoods. They halted about halfway up the mountain to listen. Utter silence! Not a bird tweeted. It was like the world was holding its breath.

"What's happening?" Chris whispered to Travis.

"The lull before the storm. Yankee troops and artillery are advancing, and our folks are blowing up the roads and causing rockslides to deny the artillery an easy way to move forward."

Chris had almost forgotten about the war. Billy Jo made a snide comment about their home being so remote that if it weren't for her, no one would have paid them any attention.

Travis called his brother to task. "You don't know that Billy Jo, and who was it that was blabbing everything to the reporter?"

It made Chris realize what a burden she and Boomer had become. The McFadden family had put themselves in danger by saving them and tending to their injuries.

The exiles rode to the top of the mountain where they could survey the narrow reddish-brown ribbon of a road where it snaked through the lower half of the mountain. It continued around the base and out of sight in the direction of the farm they had just vacated.

Chris noticed dark clouds forming below them, so dense that they obscured a large portion of the road. She urged Boomer to descend the steep grade. She wanted a closer look at the spot on the road to their right. Boomer picked his way down the incline. Chris halted him and turned to Travis. "Is that where you found us?"

"Yeah. We found y'all over that way a mite from those busted up wagon wheels. I guess the wagon was picked over by scavengers after we buried the remains of your friends.

The clouds were picking up some rotation, and Chris was able to see flashes of lightning. The rumble of thunder seemed to work like a magnet on Boomer. He began to move toward it and was oblivious to Chris's efforts to guide him. She was occupied trying to rein him in and hadn't noticed that the explosions had resumed along the road. The last thing she recalled hearing was Travis yelling for her to jump. She assumed that he meant to jump off of her horse. Instead, Chris grabbed a fistful of mane in her rein hand and squeezed with all the strength in her legs.

She held on for dear life as Boomer jumped into the cloud deck at the same moment that the dirt road beneath them blew up. Her scream was drowned out by the sounds war and the roar of the storm.

Chapter Three

Chris, once again, sat bolt upright in a strange bed while she continued to scream. Her heart rate and anxiety level were off the charts; the machines recording her condition were bleeping and buzzing. The monitor's racket, which was punctuated by her screeching, brought on a small stampede of nurses and people in white lab coats.

She made a superhuman effort to control the panic that was still permeating bone deep. A nasty male nurse threatened to strap her down and sedate her if she dislodged the contact leads again, or if she continued to wreak havoc on the collection of tubes protruding from her body. His threat gave her an added incentive to remain quiet. She glared defiantly into the squat nurse's bespectacled black eyes. It was her mom's unexpected rush to her bedside that settled her most.

She leaned down and kissed Chris on the forehead. "Christine Anne Dawson you scared me out of twenty years! I thought we were going to lose you." She hauled a chair close to her daughter's hospital bed, sat down, and took hold of her IV taped hand. "It's about time you woke up."

As Chris faded, she wondered if the nurse from hell had slipped something into one of the overhead bags that hung on a metal tree and dripped God knew what down the tube taped to the needle on the back of her hand.

She was relieved when she woke again in the hospital, and the tube down her throat that had kept her from speaking had been removed. A familiar form was changing the IV bags and adjusting the drip. "Hester?" she croaked out like a hoarse frog.

The friendly face broke into a smile. "Good to see you awake, child. How do you know my name?"

Chris noticed that the nurse's name tag only read H. Collins. R.N. "Maybe you told me, or I heard someone else use it?" she improvised. After a couple more shifts with her night nurse Chris figured out that not a soul called her Hester. Everyone, including Mom, called her Nurse Collins.

Mom looked like an older version of Chris, except that Mom didn't have a visible gray hair on her head while her daughter had a streak of white hair parting her like colored locks. It was a big joke among the aides and orderlies that the younger Dawson was the one with white hair, and there was a lot of speculation about the fact that the white patch looked like a bolt of lightning. Chris pretty much ignored them, but their weird sense of humor didn't settle well with her mother.

Chris was happy to be rid of the tubes and to be in a semi-private room instead of in ICU, but she did miss her night nurse. Mom had arrived three days prior to her awakening from the coma that she'd been in for the eight days since the accident. In this reality, the horses had been carted to a vet clinic equipped to handle them, and her companions were still alive! She wondered again about the old story of Dorothy and her little dog. Had she dreamt the whole journey back in time, as Dorothy had her trip to Oz, and projected Boomer and Hester in to her hallucination?

She went through a Twilight Zone experience a few days later when Karen came by for a visit. She was wearing a half walking cast on her right foot, but she didn't look injured otherwise.

Karen was a vivacious, strawberry-blonde and her dark blue eyes twinkled as she related the story of her father trying to operate the photo function on his phone. "Dad said that you would want to know how Boomer, Tee Jay, and Wendy are doing. He had one of the vet assistants use his phone to take a few shots of the three. Then he ordered me to upload them to share with you."

Chris thought that Mr. Russell's attempt to ease her mind about the horses was really sweet, and, unlike her friend, Chris didn't think it particularly funny. She was immensely relieved that everyone had survived the accident and figured that her recollection of the scene of the wreck when she and Boomer had climbed back up the hill was only part of her coma dream. Then she looked at the photo of the stallion's injuries. His right shoulder had a three-cornered healing scar, and his left shoulder had a jagged, lightning-shaped scar! She knew it would heal over with white hair, and an eerie sensation crawled up her back.

Karen's dad came to visit after conferring with his daughter's doctors. Karen's ankle was now pinned together. It turned out that she'd slipped on the wet pavement as she climbed from the cab of the truck and had broken her ankle. Everyone except Chris had been securely buckled up when they were hit.

Mr. Russell informed Chris that he was taking the horses, which included the new mare, and Karen back to Ohio the following morning. A silver gray GMC and matching six-horse gooseneck with living quarters was described as the new show rig. He looked at Chris and shook his head as he commented, "Could be old Tee Jay sensed the storm and the accident. We are all lucky to have survived. The next time that old horse says he doesn't want to go, I'm staying put." Her boss also informed her that Bill Jacobs was covering her mom's expenses to enable her remain with Chris until she was released. He was also footing the bill for the plane tickets back home.

She hadn't mentioned the time warp to anyone. The dates didn't coincide. To the best of her recollection, she was ejected from the truck hitting her head on the rocky ground over the guardrail. Then she woke to find Boomer standing over her, but had he really been with her or had she only imagined it? Then she remembered the photo of his wounds. How could she imagine them so vividly? Here in the hospital the calendars had only moved into the second week of June, but she'd been on board Boomer when he dove into the cloud deck on a late August afternoon. Hadn't she?

It looked like Chris was stuck with the bulky cast for at least another month. She was to have the compound break reassessed when she and her mom arrived home at the end of the week. She was more than ready to get the heck out of North Carolina, but that was prior to meeting the dark haired, blue-eyed, paramedic who had found her along the side of the mountain.

Colin McFadden appeared to be twenty-five or six, and the grown-up rendition of how she remembered Travis. In fact, when he first walked in, she called him Travis. "Sorry to disappoint you, Miss

Dawson, but Travis McFadden was my great-great-grandfather." He smiled at her, and then continued, "I'm still on shift and have to complete paperwork on the patient I transported, but I wanted to check on you."

"You know who Travis is, or was?"

"Sure, and I'll tell you the story tomorrow, if you'll have lunch with me. The cafeteria on the main floor isn't fancy, but the food is fairly good."

Chris was at a loss for words; she did the bobble-head imitation, and was only able to mutter a hoarse, "Okay."

He flashed a killer smile. "It's a date. See you at noon tomorrow." She was still nodding her head as he exited the room, and her mother entered.

Colin arrived shortly past noon the next day. He placed his laptop and a large manila envelope in her lap before pushing her mandatory wheelchair to the elevator. He escorted her to a table in a somewhat quiet corner of the crowded lunchroom. Chris allowed him pick out their meal. She was here to get some closure, or a better handle on her persistent memories of a past era. She was exercising an extraordinary amount of willpower to keep from opening the envelope or laptop that sat on the table while she waited for him to return.

He talked a bit about Travis, his ancestor, and Chris was relieved to know that Travis had actually lived and made it through the war. It seemed that the scary blonde mother of the boys was named Lucinda, and her, Confederate officer, husband was also named Colin.

"Wow! No wonder she was so bummed out by my Yankee accent." It occurred to Chris that they were talking as if her trip back in time actually happened. "I'd been doing a good job of convincing myself that the whole experience was only in my slightly dented head while in the coma. Then you show up."

"Let me show you something." He pulled out a couple of old newspaper clippings, fragile and yellowed with age. There was a photo of her on Boomer, and another of Travis, Billy Jo, their mother, and Hester. They were faded, but she recognized the people and the farm. He also pulled out some old sepia-tinted photos almost as fragile as the news clippings. "I know they aren't clear, but I wanted you to see the originals before showing you the enhanced version on the computer. The news story, which is barely legible in these clippings, is one of the files I reproduced. Billy Jo's notes, an early journal, and the book he later wrote titled "The Lightning Rider" are on the laptop, too."

"Little Billy Jo became a writer?" Chris remembered that she could barely understand the boy when he spoke. Could it be that he had found his voice in the written word?

"My understanding was that he went west and opened a newspaper office. I will leave my laptop with you so you can read it."

"Mom and I are flying home Saturday. You'll have to pick it up before then," Chris mentioned as Colin returned her to her room.

"I'm off rotation on Friday. Do you like pizza?"

"I love pizza!"

"Great. I'll bring lunch on Friday." He was barely out the door when Chris started reading the accounts about her and Boomer by the reporter whom Billy Jo had been huddled up with.

Chris was still reluctant to share her strange experience with anyone other than Colin. They would be giving her more brain scans. Maybe someday she could tell her mom about her travel through time.

On Friday, along with the pizza and Coke, Colin brought her an old wooden box with a carved lid. The carving depicted a horse and rider leaping over a bolt of lightning. Chris ran her fingers over it several times. "Open it," Colin urged her.

Inside were a couple of dollar bills and some change that she had stuck in the pocket of her jeans before loading the horses for that fateful trip. The coins were discolored with age, and the bills were as fragile as the hand-written note included with her money, all of which had twenty-first century mint dates.

Chris,

Hester found the script and coins when she cleaned and repaired your trousers. I swore to her that I would return this strange currency to our favorite Yankee invader.

I sure hope you and that crazy cloud jumping horse made it back safely. We kind of miss you around here.

Forever your friend,

Travis

When she finished reading the note, she carefully folded it before placing it in the box. She tried to return it to Colin, but he refused to take it. Instead, he handed her a plastic bag before he snagged another slice of pizza.

Chris' mom had been watching the interaction between them with a good deal of interest while she enjoyed a slice of pepperoni pizza.

"Colin, I can't keep this; it's been in your family for more than a century."

"We were only its caretakers. It was made for you. I knew who you were as soon as I worked my way down the mountain to find you at the feet of your lightning horse, and holding onto the reins in that bag."

Chris opened the bag to find the cloth halter and reins she had woven from remnants gathered by her friends back in 1863.

A RAINY NIGHT

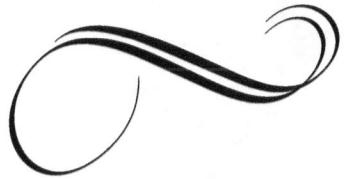

J D sat on the front stoop of Joan Curtis' little house enjoying the soft summer rain. He was also looking back over the last few days with Cassie and lost opportunities to get closer to her. He'd spent a large part of the afternoon at the barn with her helping move her tack into the assigned locker that matched Bucky's stall number. Once her new horse was settled, they returned home to escort her grandmother to church. He offered to take them out for dinner, but Cassie refused to go unless she paid for the meal. She was making him crazy! She wasn't interested in the money that her father had left her, nor did she want anything to do with the ranch.

It was raining harder now. *This is sure a different world from the one I grew up in, he thought, or the stinking desert where I will soon be deployed. My third tour of Iraq facing me, and I hate the place more with each return. Even when I'm not in the war-zone it stays with me. I can't sit on a step in the rain on a quiet dead end street without feeling that someone is lurking in the dark corners where the streetlights don't reach.*

More and more of his sleep was disrupted by haunting images of white hot heat radiating of the desert sand and pockmarked white buildings. Eyes tracked his unite's progress as they patrolled the streets and alleyways. Were they the wary eyes of the innocent inhabitants, frightened out of their wits, or were they the intent stares of insurgent snipers?

He gave himself a mental shake, but still couldn't shake the feeling that he was being observed. All thought fled when Cassie stepped out the door behind him.

Rain beating on the asphalt shingles woke Casey with an urgent need to relieve her bladder. The change in the weather had her head feeling like a balloon ready to burst, so she checked for her stash of ibuprofen. "Oh, crap!" She was all out of her supply and grumbled, "I guess I'll have to try down stairs. Maybe Gram has a store of aspirin in the first floor bath medicine cabinet." She worked her way down to the main floor without turning on the lights. The night-lights in the hall, bathroom, and kitchen helped her navigate. With pills on their way into her system targeting her throbbing sinuses, she refilled her glass from the water dispenser on the fridge. On her way back to her room, she noticed the open front door. Geeze, Gram you are really slipping! She was thinking that her grandmother's decline could be worse than she thought. She was pondering how to get Gram's belligerent fanny to the doctor for a checkup.

She saw him sitting on the front stoop, shirtless and barefoot, as she was about to close and lock up. Instead, she opened the screen door and sat on the step beside him. "What are you doing out here?"

"Just enjoying the rain."

Something was bothering him, and she figured he was unable to sleep. "Well…it's a good thing it's the middle of the night. Otherwise 911 would be overrun with calls from women on this end of Frank Street complaining of heart palpitations."

"What about you? That tee shirt barely reaches mid-thigh! Do you run around out here dressed like that often?"

She wanted to smack him. It was his fault she was out here in her nightshirt. Casey decided to change the subject. "You're not doing it right."

"Doing what right."

"The whole rain thing!"

He'd no idea what she was talking about and was about to ask for clarification when she set her water glass on the stoop, walked onto the lawn, and began twirling in the rain. This wasn't the little girl performing at a dance recital, but a pagan goddess that could be a serious contender in a wet t-shirt contest!

Casey held out her arms to him. "Come on, Jimmy boy, haven't you ever danced in the rain?"

He was finding it hard to control his physical response to her erotic rain dance. "Can't say that I ever have."

She walked up and took hold of his hands, "Well, it's about time you gave it a try!"

A very short time later the thought occurred to her: maybe she should have left him on the front porch. What started out as a couple dancing a simple two-step in the rain quickly turned into a carnal embrace.

JD lifted Casey off her feet and kissed her. He'd wanted to hold her and kiss her ever since he had seen her in Denver, but this unexpected encounter was getting out of hand! All reasonable thought left him when she put her arms around his neck and instigated a tongue-thrusting kiss.

Casey's female core responded to him like it had never done to anyone before. She couldn't get close enough to him. When he cupped her butt urging her close to his erection she opened her legs to wrap them around him.

"What are you children doing out in the pouring rain?"

Oh God! It was Gram! Casey disengaged her grip on JD the instant he took his hands off her, and she went tumbling to the soggy lawn in a fit of laughter.

"Casey, stop acting like a crazy person before the neighbors call the police! Come in the side door; I don't want you kids tracking up my living room carpet."

Kids? Oh boy, here we go again, she thought. "I hope she doesn't forget to open the side door; she just closed and locked this one."

JD didn't say a word, but waited for her to pick up her glass. Then he took her arm as they crossed the lawn and worked their way up the drive to the now unlocked side entrance.

Gram was waiting for them on the landing just inside the entry. "Go downstairs and towel off, while I make you some hot chocolate. I ought to take a switch to both of you. You'll be lucky if you don't come down with pneumonia!"

Casey flicked on the basement light and went straight to the dryer to pull out a couple of fresh towels. Armed with a clean shirt and a pair of boxer shorts, she changed in the small gray tiled bathroom.

"I'll run up and get you a clean pair of britches. Use the shower if you want. I'll be right back."

His dress uniform was hung in the closet of the guest room, but everything that he had worn in the past few days was stuffed into a large plastic bag in his duffel. She pulled out the dirty laundry and located a clean pair of briefs as well as a pair of jeans. She carried it all down stairs receiving a quelling look of disapproval as she passed her grandmother. Casey knocked on the bathroom door. "Throw out the wet trousers and I'll give you the dry ones." He threw out the wet jeans and took the dry offerings. She picked up the wet jeans. "Is that it?"

"Yeah. Unless you want the towels too."

"No. I'll get them later with the rest of the linens." Lord, she thought, he didn't have any underwear on, and neither did I! If it hadn't been for Gram's timely interruption she could be in a world of hurt. She'd be willing to bet he didn't have a condom handy. She surely hadn't, nor had the use of birth control even entered her mind. She threw his mixed load of laundry in the washer and set the temperature selector to cold. She trudged up the stairs like a kid who'd been caught with her hand in a cookie jar; JD was right behind her.

Gram plunked a mug of hot chocolate, complete with mini marshmallows, in front of each on them. Dressed in a pink flannel nightgown and matching quilted robe, she sat down at the table with her own mug and lowered the boom. "I'm really disappointed in both of you. My granddaughter cavorting in the rain like some kind of demented wood nymph! As for you young man, you have almost a decade on her and should know better."

"Yes Mama. Sorry Mama, it won't happen again."

Casey lost it and broke into another fit of laughter. Gram got up and smacked her! That reprimand only made her laugh harder. Smack! At that point JD protested, "Honestly, Mrs. Curtis, the whole thing was as much my fault as Cassie's."

"See! So, why don't you go smack Jimmy in the chops?"

"Because he apologized for his inappropriate behavior, you naughty girl, and I don't doubt for an instant that you instigated the whole episode."

What could she say? She really did start the fireworks with her silly rain dance. The washer completed its cycle and saved her any more verbal abuse. She folded the rest of the towels and other personal items that were in the dryer before putting JD's things in.

She heard them in deep conversation, though she couldn't make out the words over the mechanical workings of the dryer. She curled up in her grandpa's old recliner that had long ago been relegated to the bowels of the house. She pulled the faded green lap robe from the back of the like colored La-Z-Boy to ward off the chills wracking her body.

A short while later, Casey watched JD descend the stairs with a mug in each hand; she covertly wiped the tears with the ancient afghan. He offered her one of the mugs, and then pulled out an old armchair that matched the recliner. JD positioned it so he would be facing her.

"What are you doing down here, Cassie?"

She sipped the hot chocolate before answering. "I'm waiting for the dryer to stop. I imagine you will want to pack your clean clothing before you leave this morning."

"You did my laundry?"

He sounded incredulous. "Why does that shock you? I'm quite capable of performing the daily humdrum of domestic chores."

"I didn't mean it that way. It's only that I've been doing for myself for a very longtime. Thank you."

FLASH FLOOD
TEXAS STYLE

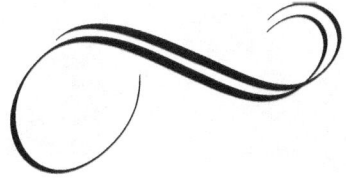

Alexandra, reluctantly, started on the trip to Decker's place on a bright sunny afternoon. An hour north of Lubbock, the sun had gone into hiding behind some ominous black clouds. She felt the same sense of foreboding that she had experienced upon her first encounter with David Decker. She and Melinda had just checked into their shared suite when David appeared out of the blue. She knew that Melinda must have told him of their impending arrival. Lexie made the first designated turn on her route, piloting Melinda's graduation gift onto a gravel road. The Escalade bit into the gravel and traveled the mile and a quarter without incident. Her written instructions and the GPS were in agreement so far. Another half-hour and she came to fork where she turned left onto a rutted dirt road, and that was when it started to rain. She slipped the large SUV into four-wheel drive and turned the wipers on low. All that accomplished was to make a mess of the accumulated dust on the windshield, but several squirts of the washer fluid cleared a small spot for her to see where she was going.

Her mood was as dark as the clouds that had taken over a previously bright blue sky. Texas hadn't looked much different to her when she exited the Interstate upon their arrival, but she had been feeling ill and not paying much attention. Scenery blurred by at seventy miles an hour as they had traveled the homogenous interstate system that offered the same fast food joints, chain restaurants, and box stores from coast to coast. Lexie had opted to drive most of the trip. It was easier for her to control bouts of carsickness when she was in control of the vehicle and was required to concentrate on traffic and road signs. She'd only vaguely taken notice of the absence of green as they entered Oklahoma with its endless fields of grasshopper-like oil pumping rigs. Her perception of the Texas panhandle underwent a drastic change once she left the relative safety of the hotel parking lot in Lubbock to join Melinda and her heartthrob for dinner.

She applied the brakes at another fork in the road in the road that was not on the written instructions or the GPS. *So much for back-up!* The SUV skidded in the slime now covering the previously dry, dusty, road. Lexie retrieved her phone from an inside pocket of her navy colored, leather, handbag. Disgusted, she laid it on the center console. Smart or not, the directional phone apps had not shed any light on her dilemma. She was really beginning to feel lousy, so she twisted of the cap on the antibiotic that she had just picked up at the drugstore. The prescription label said it was to be taken with food, but she was desperate to head of a recurrence of what sure felt like the flu, so she downed the pill with the remainder of a bottle of water she'd placed in the cup holder. Lexie picked up the small communication device, located Melinda's name, and poked the small screen much harder than required to connect to her friend. She wanted to scream! *Why me Lord?* Melinda didn't have a clue how to direct her. While her friend checked with David, she slipped into her navy jacket. As the rain increased, the heat of earlier began to cool, and she was experiencing a chill. Lexie switched from the air conditioner to the heater.

She was sitting in the middle of a dirt road in an increasing rain, and the surface was quickly becoming a quagmire. She hoped that Melinda was writing down directions and that was why she was taking so much time.

Roommates since their freshman year at Ohio State, Alexandra Parker and Melinda Potter had become close friends. After nearly five years, their friendship had grown to the point they each knew the other's personality quirks. Lexie knew Melinda well enough to be skeptical about the accuracy of the written directions that her friend had left for her when she went on ahead with David. Commonsense had dictated that she enter his ranch address in the GPS, just in case.

Finally, Melinda was back on the phone, and in the nick of time. Lexie felt the Cadillac sinking into the softening road surface while she had been impatiently waiting for further directions.

"Lexie? David says to take the left fork. He says that you are only about a mile from the house."

"A mile in this stuff might just as well be a hundred."

"Quit complaining, Lexie, just put the Escalade in four-wheel drive and you will be alright. See you in a bit."

Lexie didn't answer her. Instead, she just threw her phone onto the console. Aggravated with herself for agreeing to this trip, she rolled the vehicle forward. Mud flew and the vehicle fishtailed a little, but the tires found purchase. Less than a quarter of a mile crawled by until the road suddenly disappeared into a roaring creek. With nowhere to turn around, she began backing over her tracks. Progress was slow. The small single wiper on the rear window made it difficult to navigate through the increasing downpour. She could hear Melinda's voice in her mind *David says, David says*. She gave herself a mental shake, and concentrated on reverse driving.

Back out on the dirt road, she made a decision to take the right fork. If her mind was functioning past her blinding headache, she recalled that back the way she had come the same previously dry creek that flooded the left fork also ran under a culvert on the main dirt excuse for a road. By now, it too was probably washed out. The right fork rose on a very slight incline and promised higher ground. She was thinking that higher ground might keep her from drowning, but the mud was getting deeper. Lexie was worried about getting bogged down in the middle of nowhere. Most likely, any help she could summon from her friend could not reach her in time. She had the wipers up full force, and was driving even slower to avoid sliding off the edge. The right fork spilt again about a mile from the last divide. Once more, she picked the option with the potential for higher elevation. She proceeded at a snail's pace with her vehicle now in low gear as she squinted through the windshield into the growing monsoon. She followed a curve in the road, and a large shadow suddenly loomed in front of her. It occupied the center of the road. Lexie swerved to avoid what looked to be a large animal and slid smack into the muck at the right side of the road.

She felt the Escalade sink! Her temper broke the tenuous hold she had on it. She turned off the engine and barreled out the driver's side door. So intent on venting her frustration on the huge cow that blocked the road, she forgot that she wearing her navy dress pumps. The cow was the recipient of the frustration she couldn't vent on Melinda and her creepy Romeo. David Decker was attractive enough physically with his black wavy hair, cornflower blue eyes, and an engaging smile, but there was something sinister about the man. Lexie sank in six inches of muck, and with the next step her shoes were buried in it.

"Are you in a hurry to be hamburger? I could have run you over in this blinding rain! Now, look, you've killed the damned Cadillac." The beast wouldn't move out of the road. Pushing on its rump didn't accomplish anything, nor did smacking it on the hip. That little bout of temper left her with a stinging hand. The white face was halterless—*it's not a horse,* she reminded herself—and she didn't have a rope or even a belt. Now nearly knee-deep in slop, she stood there, hands on her hips, glaring at the cow. While she was assessing the situation, the cow let out a bellow. A small echo bounced back from a few feet away. Lexie spotted a small calf stuck in the mud. All that was visible was the head and a small portion of its back. The little one was sinking in a run-off of muck that had flowed from the slightly higher terrain behind it.

Now the *no rope or belt* thing was a real dilemma. Improvising, she removed her navy jacket that had matched her now trashed slacks. Lexie waded closer to the calf, hoping she didn't sink along with it. Keeping a wary eye on its watchful mother, she slipped the jacket around the calf's neck and gave a tug. She managed to raise its head a little higher, but it was stuck and could not get any traction to assist in its rescue attempt. Giving a little stronger tug, she lost her own traction. She was sitting on her butt in the mud, propping up the small creature's head. Lexie was in danger of sinking in the muck along with the baby cow when the ghost riders just appeared from out of the storm.

One minute, no one was around for miles, and then — poof — there they were. *Maybe I am hallucinating?* She was trying hard to focus, but her head was throbbing and she was beginning to shake uncontrollably. Through the veil of rain, one rider looked like a normal person as they rode closer. He sat astride a sorrel-colored cowpony with a white star, but that was about all that she could tell. From the belly down, both horses were thick with mud that had splashed higher up on the animals; their riders' legs were in much the same condition. Both horsemen wore black Stetsons and outback-type oilskin dusters. The dark cowboy was bigger than the other man and was mounted on a, large, coal-black stallion. It was he who brought forth the image of a ghost rider.

"You need some help, little girl?" His voice was a low baritone, close to a bass, with a thick Texan drawl. She was feeling a bit weak from her trek through the mud and trying to free the calf. It was hard to decipher his words through the roaring in her ears and unrelenting rain. He repeated the question as he rode closer and dismounted.

All she could say was, "He is drowning in the mud."

Without another word the dark rider caught a loop from the other cowboy's rope and replaced her jacket with the rope before he picked her up out of the mud. He unceremoniously deposited her by the side of her vehicle while he returned to the hapless calf. Gratefully, she leaned against the bogged-down Cadillac for support. Her head was beginning to swim, and a bone-shattering chill had over taken her, but Lexie realized that she was no longer shivering as she had been sitting in the runoff with the newborn calf. *This can't be good,* she thought. *Maybe my body is shutting down?* She watched the tall cowboy wade into the mud hole and lift the backend of the calf, while the rider on the sorrel backed his horse giving a steady tug on the rope. In no time, momma cow and baby were on higher ground, and wandering back to their herd.

Her mind registered that she was way overdue for her dinner invitation. She reached in the still open door for her phone. It was time to call Melinda and tell her to have dinner without her. The phone had fallen to the floor near the gas pedal when she had swerved, and ditched the expensive SUV. She leaned in to retrieve it smearing mud on the light gray leather interior. Once she latched on to it and righted herself in the driver side bucket seat, her efforts to manipulate the small phone with her muddy hands sent it right through her grip. Lexie watched in disbelief as her iPhone took a dive out the open door and sank into the muck. *That's the last straw!* "I knew I should have just stayed in Lubbock," she grumbled to the fast disappearing phone. It was now buried in the same muddy grave as her navy pumps.

This is just terrific! I am supposed to be the stabilizing influence according to Melinda's parents. It was they who had convinced her that she needed a break after the stress of finals. Mrs. Potter insisted that Lexie needed a rest to spring back from her run-down condition following a nasty bout of the flu, and Lexie's mother had agreed with Linda Potter.

Lexie'd been aware that Melinda's e-mails to David Decker, and his to her had been getting pretty steamy. What she hadn't known was that Melinda was planning on traveling to Texas after graduation to meet her Internet dating service's most recent match. Lexie was losing her tenuous hold on reality as she slid down into the mud against the side of the muck covered, once white Escalade, giving up the search for her phone and shoes.

Most of the herd was up closer to the ranch out of harm's way for the moment, and they had been rounding up the inevitable strays when the forecasted rains hit. The remnants of tropical storms seldom made it this far north, but when they did, flash floods often resulted. All the cattle were accounted for except the big Hereford cow ready to drop a late calf. They'd left the other hands to move the rounded up strays toward the relative safety of the ranch. Cutter, the owner of the outfit and his foreman, Jim Rodriguez, went in search of the old cow. They had a hunch where she would be, and under most circumstances it wouldn't have worried them. She liked to drop her calves down near the water. Today, it could prove deadly if she sought an isolated spot near there to deliver.

Cutter was exhausted having only returned from four days in Dallas late that morning. He'd not even unpacked when he joined the rest of his crew to move the cattle away from potential flash flood areas.

Riding in the midst of a torrential downpour and several inches of mud made for slow progress. By the time they approached the spot where they figured the expectant cow would seek solitude, the river was emitting an earsplitting roar. A larger object entered Cutter's peripheral as they continued to scan the surroundings for their missing bovine. Jim saw it about the same time and let loose with a string of cuss words that sizzled out into another cloudburst. A large white, mud covered, vehicle was rounding the curve and about to run down his pregnant Hereford. Too far away to holler a warning, they waited for the inevitable collision, but the driver swerved at the last moment and sank that fancy rig to its rocker panels.

Some days it paid unexpected dividends to battle the elements. Neither he nor Jim would ever forget watching the driver, dressed like one of those professional women on the TV, exit like she was ready for a fight. Then she rounded on mamma cow. She was hollering at it and giving it a piece of her mind while trying to push it out of the road. She even smacked it on the rump. Mamma cow let out a threat of her own, and the little lady backed off. *No.* Cutter thought *It wasn't the cow's threat that stopped her assault, but something else that had caught her attention.* Both cattlemen knew what had distracted her was most likely a newborn calf. As they rode closer they watched as she pulled off her jacket, wrapped it around the calf's neck, then sat or fell down beside it. She remained there, propping that small head above the mud, and sinking along with it!

The mud-covered woman stared at him as if he were the headless horseman. He had to ask her twice if she needed some help. With Jim's rope securely around the small critter to keep its head above the mud hole, he plucked the calf's would-be rescuer out of the deepening mud and set her on her feet by the Cadillac. Then he went back to help Jim haul the newborn out of the mud. Jim took the calf up across his lap and rode a safe distance from the rising water before releasing it. The calf was none the worse for its experience, largely due to the little lady keeping its head elevated.

Cutter turned around to check on her. He was amazed to see her sitting in the mud with her back propped against the side of her mud-splattered ride. She continued looking at him as if her were the devil incarnate. He approached her slowly. Her up swept hairdo was falling down on one side. He estimated that soaking wet and covered in mud she couldn't weigh more than a hundred pounds. The continuing down pour had rinsed the heavy mud from her soaked once white silk blouse; it clung to her petite form affording an enticing peek at a lacy bra that barely hid her pert breasts. Obviously chilled her nipples were puckered and erect. Cutter needed to get a grip on himself and stop ogling the stranded little woman with the mistrustful blue eyes.

He took precious moments to walk around the vehicle as far as possible and wipe off the front license plate that declared the Cadillac was from Ohio. Curiosity took hold. "Are you lost?"

"What makes you think I am lost, cowboy?"

Her voice was an octave above a whisper, shaky and thin, but she definitely had a Yankee accent. He tried again, "I'm Cutter. What's your name?" She looked at him as if he was speaking a foreign language.

"I lost it."

"You lost your name?" *She wasn't making any sense.*

"Of course not. I lost my shoes, and my phone, not to mention a mangy cow killed my car, but I haven't lost my name." She spoke to him as if he were a little slow on the uptake.

Okay, he thought, I'll give it one more try.

"My name is Alexandra," she volunteered, before he could ask again. It was obvious she didn't trust him.

It could be she had caught me scrutinizing her physical attributes. Cutter tried to be patient with her, but the nearby stream was quickly becoming a raging torrent, and he couldn't let her stay where she was.

"Alexandra, we need to move away from here, or we are both going to drown." She just shook her head looking at his big black stallion with huge terrified blue eyes when he suggested that she mount his horse to ride out of there with him. He took the decision out of her hands. The rising water was lapping at the right side of the Cadillac, and they were out of time. Cutter plucked her out of the mud, one more time, and carried her over to deposit her on his saddle. She had the presence of mind to straddle it, and he quickly mounted behind her, spurring Rowdy to higher ground. Her silk blouse clung to her small frame, and she shivered uncontrollably. Opening his duster, he pulled her close to him and closed the front over her. She objected at first, but then relented out of concern for Rowdy when Cutter scolded her, "Quit wiggling. You're making it harder for my horse to pick his way through this muck." She settled down immediately. He'd expected her to be cold when he pulled her against him, and he'd been concerned about hyperthermia. Of even more concern was the fact that she was burning up and becoming lethargic. He figured it would probably be a good idea to get her to focus by talking to him.

"Alexandra? I'll bet that they call you Alex." Her voice was fading and becoming weaker, but she responded.

"Wrong. My friends call me Lexie. However, you can call me Alexandra."

He suppressed the urge to laugh. He had a hunch that under normal circumstances, she was a handful. "What were you doing out here Alexandra?"

"Playing in the mud with your cows. They were your cows, weren't they?"

"Yep, they're mine. You like cows, Alexandra?"

"I like them just fine, served up as a medium rare porterhouse."

Her response surprised Cutter, given the effort that she had put forth to save the calf, and he told her so. "You must really like steak, to jump in the mud with a potential dinner."

"Well...it's just a baby. You really ought to make hamburger out of that cow once the baby is weaned."

"You don't think she would make good steaks?" "She doesn't deserve to be steaks. She is a lousy mother, parking her baby in the middle of a road. It is like a human telling their kids to go play in traffic."

WICKED WINDS

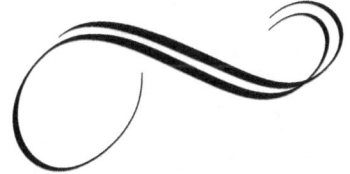

Chapter One
1980 Flight

A torrential downpour made visibility nearly impossible as I piloted my recently acquired used car south on Tennessee 31 and struggled to keep my hands from shaking. My grip on the steering wheel had passed the white knuckle stage, and my eyes were watering from the constant strain of peering through the heavy rain. Wipers worked feverishly to battle the onslaught, but I could barely make out the white hood of my little Dodge Dart. Since the hood of my car seemed to melt into storm, I was hoping perhaps the rest of the car would be equally cloaked by the rain.

"There it is!" My cousin, Lynn, hollered from the passenger seat. She shouted to be heard above the road noise and thunder. I had almost passed the on ramp to I-65.

If my calculations were correct, we were in Alabama. Prior to this insanity, my dog-eared road atlas showed State 31 intersecting with I-65 in Alabama near the Tennessee line.

"What now?" Lynn asked, as if she expected me to know!

I improvised. "We'll stay on the Interstate to put some distance between us and Tennessee. Take a look at the map, Lynn. Try to locate a likely spot fifty to a hundred miles south where we can fill the tank and get something to eat. We will need to change direction from there and get off the Interstate. It is the first place they will look for us, and every truck is a potential enemy scout."

The rain was letting up as we traveled south, but the strong winds occasionally rocked my little Dart and threatened to blow us off the highway. I was praying for an exit before we drew any attention should a few errant truckers be on the highway. I never figured that my initial visit with my cousin would end up with us racing south and running for our lives.

Lynn and her little son, Trevor, were working on their burgers and fries when I joined them. I'd stashed the Dart around the back of the building between a couple of large campers; I hoped their owners didn't leave before we did. I was cold and miserable, not to mention scared out of my mind, and the chicken dumpling soup sounded like just the ticket.

We were sharing another cup of coffee while going over the road atlas and planning the next stage of our escape. At that point in time, a uniformed law officer entered in the company of what appeared to be a cowboy in a dark rain slicker. Lynn was losing it. "Do you think they are looking for us?" she whispered.

I tried to reassure her. "I think they're only having something to eat." The law could very well have a description of us and Trevor if her lunatic husband had reported his son as missing. My cousin was terrified the police officer would detain us until Bobby Jo and his half-wit brother, Henry, could catch up with us. "Lynn, why don't you and Trevor use the restroom before we leave while I pay the bill? We won't be able to stop again for quite a while. I'll pick up some donuts and coffee to go."

I was pocketing my change and about to pick up the carryout containers when Lynn exited the restroom with Trevor in tow. She glanced toward the main door of the truck stop, and then let loose with an earsplitting screech.

"Jack! They've found us."

"Go back into the restroom." After offering that lame bit of advice, I asked for a cup of coffee and had the girl at the checkout stash our order behind the counter. From my swivel stool at the counter, I watched the door behind me through the mirrored back of the donut and pastry display.

I picked up the heavy glass sugar dispenser and freely poured the contents into the hot brew. My hands were shaking violently, so a good amount of sugar decorated the counter. I sure didn't need the distraction of the tall imposing cowboy who was now paying his check, but he just wandered back to join his companion. I was a bit unnerved when he responded to the panicked bellow of my name.

Henry Bodine entered the restaurant; he paused to scan the patrons and staff. I had the distinct feeling that he was stalling. So, where was Bobby Jo? He had to be here too. Henry walked up behind me and growled. "Get up. We're leaving, or do you want to die here?"

Neither of his choices appealed to me, but I decided I would rather die here than let him torture me to death. I threw my thick coffee mixture over my shoulder in the direction of his face. It was obvious from the howl of pain that my aim had been dead on. Henry was busy trying to wipe the goo out of his eyes. I spun around on the stool with the sugar container in hand and planted it upside his head. He staggered back from me. Still seated on the stool, I kicked him in his family jewels. As he hit the floor, I leapt over his prone form with the intention of locating Lynn and Trevor. Then the three of us needed to get the hell out of Dodge!

He managed to snag my pant leg as I attempted to clear his body. I went down hard. Lynn's terrified scream was ringing in my ears as the world went black.

Chapter Two
Forces of Nature

April 27, 2011

All hell broke loose in North and Central Alabama that Wednesday. Three waves of tornados wreaked havoc on the residents of Cullman County. Jack Hargrove was one of the first responders to reach those injured in the wake of the F 4 and 5 monsters that leveled homes, businesses, and claimed lives. Shelters needed to be set up for the homeless. The devastation was extensive.

Jack was exhausted. He'd gone without sleep for nearly fifty hours, and he still couldn't verify the whereabouts of his family. His wife of thirty years had gone to visit their daughter at the University of Alabama in Tuscaloosa a few days prior to the epic tornado outbreak. Communications were spotty at best with the power still out. Cell towers were leveled along with power lines. Uprooted trees and debris from structures littered roads and highways. Many state and federal buildings across Alabama and neighboring states were damaged or wiped off their foundations.

Folding his arms on his desk, he rested his head on them. A thought crossed his mind; his wife was like a force of nature. She could be all sunny, sweetness, and light, but when she got riled up, a smart man stayed out of her path. He recalled the storm from the north that changed his life nearly thirty-one years earlier.

June 1980

He had taken a long overdue vacation and gone to the family farm to visit with his parents. Jack worked on the place whenever he could and contributed funds for a hired hand in his absence. He wanted to do more, but his job was time consuming. And to be honest, his mom drove him to distraction. He was thirty-five, and every time he visited she gave him the third degree. "Seeing anyone special?"

He would tell her something on the order of, "They're all special." His dad would chuckle, and his wife of fifty years would quell him with a disapproving look.

The drive back would have suited the outboard that he and his dad used for fishing more than his Jimmy. The truck was great on back roads and cross-country, but nothing was immune to this monsoon. Half of an hour after picking up the Interstate south, he exited I-65 and pulled into the truck stop where he was to meet Carter for an update on events during his time off. He was looking forward to a meal, some good strong coffee, and conversation that wouldn't end with nagging about his solitary lifestyle.

Carter switched off the CB he'd been monitoring, locked the cruiser, and stepped into the rain.

"Howdy, Carter." Jack pulled his Stetson lower on his brow, and a small stream rolled off the brim to trail down the front of his oilskin slicker. The rain was letting up a bit as they entered the restaurant section of the sprawling truck stop.

Jack scanned the area as they made their way to the fourth booth to the right. It afforded them a view of not only the restaurant, but also the attached store and the front parking lot. The building was constructed in a circular floor plan. Six booths lined the large windows flanking the entry to the right. The two booths behind them, facing toward the store, were unoccupied, and truckers appeared to be the diners in the first three. Windows continued to the left of where they had entered, which allowed customers of those four booths a similar view of the parking area. The first booth was vacant, the second had two teen couples in animated conversation while working on burgers and fries, the third needed to be bussed, and the fourth was filled with thirty-something women in professional attire. Carter commented that they were most likely in route to or from a seminar.

A large corner booth with a round table made up the first of six booths down the side toward the ladies restroom and showers. The second booth down the wall seated two couples that Jack estimated to be in their sixties. The next in line was filled with dirty tableware and the tip was still on the table. Two young women and a small boy were in booth four. The next two also needed to be cleaned off. Two free standing tables ran down that side and could be combined for a large party. Only the first table seated patrons, a young man, a blonde woman, and a small child in a junior chair.

One of the truckers occupying stools at the counter opposite Jack and Carter's booth got up to check out at the cash register that sat at the end of the counter, which faced a donut case on the back wall. The entry to the kitchen was at the opposite end of the counter. Jack sat facing the store and souvenir area. He'd noticed several travelers come and go. The men's restroom and showers were located at the back of the store. The staff was able to access either restroom from the rear of the kitchen where the dishwashers worked.

The two waitresses on the floor had to buss their own tables. The woman behind the counter served customers seated there, filled orders to go, and cashed out the diners.

"Busy night," Carter commented. "A lot of folks waiting out the storm."

Jack nodded at his companion's observation. Carter's military hair cut offset his soft, doe like, brown eyes. His neat sandy hair made Jack realize how long his own dark locks had grown. His eyes were a blue that sometimes looked glacial. The men stood eye to eye, but Jack figured that Carter had another inch on his own six foot three. Both men were tough and fit, which came in handy in their line of work.

Carter continued to update him on happenings in the county since he had taken his leave.

"Sounds pretty tame," Jack stated. "Maybe, I should take time off more often."

"My turn next Jack." Carter took a sip of the refilled coffee and waited for the waitress to move off. "I was monitoring nineteen on the CB while waiting for you. There was some chatter about a child abduction, which included instructions to turn to channel nine for updates and descriptions. A four-year-old child was abducted from his home in Tennessee by his mother and an accomplice. Word is they're traveling in an older model Dodge Dart with Ohio plates. The car is being described as white or tan and believed headed south."

"Did you check with any of our people or the State Patrol?'

"The Highway Patrol said that no alerts had been passed to them, but one of their northern posts was also monitoring the news. Strange thing, the discrepancy in that alert reported the car headed north. Descriptions of the wife, child, and accomplice weren't included in any of the transmissions."

"You know, Carter, it sounds like someone is hunting on their own and using the truckers as their eyes. Did you see anything like a Dart when you pulled in?"

"No, but I was pretty busy tracking info. Tennessee HP didn't have any reports of child abductions either."

The two men finished their meal and kept their eyes open as cars drove in and over toward the fuel pumps; they were scanning for a light colored Dart. They paid acute attention to the man and woman who rose from the table and lifted a small boy from his seat. About the same time, one of the women from the side booth got up and took a small boy to the ladies' room.

The man and woman with the child left in a dark Chevy Suburban. Both men relaxed. Jack picked up the check. "I'll catch it this time."

The waitress behind the counter was bringing out an order for the girl in front of him when someone yelled his name. The panic in the woman's voice was evident. "WHAT!" He barked at the same instant the dark haired girl in front of him asked that very question. Surprised at his response, the brunette glanced up, and he saw the same panic in her hazel eyes that he had heard in the other woman's voice. It was a fleeting impression. She recovered in the blink of an eye. Her voice was ultra-calm when she issued the order for the blonde woman to take the child and hide in the restroom while she tried to distract them. Then, she took a seat at the counter.

Jack took note of her dumping half of the sugar canister into her mug of hot coffee. The little brunette who shared his name barely reached his shoulder height. She was probably a hundred pounds soaking wet, her hands were trembling, and she wasn't nearly as calm as her voice had indicated. Jack paid the cashier before returning to the booth to coordinate with Carter. "Keep your eyes open. I'm going to sit on the other side of the entry where I can watch your back and have a clearer view of the store and ladies' room. Something is going down."

He walked over and sat in the second booth that the teens had just vacated. Jack watched the kids track across the parking lot. A surly looking farmer type wearing bib overalls and a red flannel shirt plowed through the group of young people.

Jack noticed the way the brunette was watching the door reflected in the mirror behind the counter. She grasped her coffee mug in both hands, like people do when they are cold and trying to warm up. He knew as soon as the guy entered that the women had reason to be terrified. The man looked to be about his own height and nearly three hundred pounds of pure meanness. His soulless black eyes peered out from beneath a bushy set of brows that matched his beard and straight shoulder length hair.

Jack was looking for other players to this drama. The blonde woman had said "They have found us," so he figured there had to be at least one more. He didn't have to speculate long. A scream from the restroom had him on his feet with his service revolver in his hand. A slightly cleaner and leaner version of the other man burst out of the restroom. He evidently was usually clean shaven, but this night he sported a heavy five o'clock shadow. He held the blonde before him, like a shield, with a gun pointed at her head. It was obvious that the woman was pregnant and just as evident that the small child clinging to her skirts was scared to death.

Bobby Jo had entered before his brother and worked his way around through the kitchen; he had heard Lynn's cousin tell her to hide with his son.

Carter glanced at the second arrival, but figured that Jack could handle him. He hadn't detected any additional threats, so he returned his attention to the one approaching the girl at the counter. She sure gave the impression of being unconcerned. She sat there and ignored him until he reached for her. At that point, she shared her hot, syrupy coffee with his bearded face, spun around on the stool, and hit him so hard with the sugar canister that it shattered. As he staggered back she attempted a fifty yard field goal with his balls! The moron rolled on the floor and produced a six inch blade as he snagged the girl's leg when she tried to leap over him.

Carter kicked the knife from his hand, pointed his revolver at his head, and used similar words to those the knife wielder used to threaten the girl. "On your stomach, tough guy. Hands behind your head, or die right here." Carter cuffed him, and then he turned his attention to the girl.

Everything went down fast once the little girl made her bid for freedom. Bobby Jo yelled, "Henry, gut the bitch and get it over with." His order to his brother brought the blonde to life. She attempted to claw her captor's face; at the same instant, she shoved the child toward Jack.

Jack had moved closer to his half of the deadly duo while the guy was distracted by Carter's takedown of his partner. Jack intercepted the hand off of the little boy and pulled the child behind him. "Put the gun down and release the woman."

Bobby Jo responded with a threat to his hostage. "Back off, hero, and hand over my son unless you want to see her brains blown out."

The gunman was beyond reason. Jack could see it in his crazy dark eyes. "Sorry, but I'm the sheriff in these parts and can't just let you walk." The blonde went limp, as if she'd fainted, and Jack's bullet hit Bobby Jo between the eyes. The blond never glanced at her dead husband; she scooped up her bawling son and made a beeline toward the other girl. The child was crying "Auntie Jack, Auntie Jack!" His mother let out a pitiful cry as she knelt beside the other girl

"Don't move her." Carter warned the distraught woman.

Jack knelt on the other side of the girl who shared his name to keep her still. Obviously, the distress in her cousin's voice and the child's sobbing worried her. She attempted to sit up. "Stay quiet, the threat is over, your cousin and nephew are safe, and an ambulance is on the way."

Jack had called in the State Patrol. Then he locked down the truck stop. No one went out or in once the ambulance departed with the two women and the boy. Jack wanted outside corroboration early in the investigation. He was responsible for a fatal shooting, and Carter was his deputy. The body was on the floor covered with a tablecloth, and Henry was sitting up in the same spot where Carter had cuffed him. Carter kept an eye on Henry, who had been quite docile since the demise of his brother.

Chapter Three
Sorting Out The Players

The State Patrol secured the scene of the shooting; statements were taken from customers and staff before they hauled Henry off to jail. Bobby Jo Bodine was taking up space at the morgue. His widow was the well stacked blonde with the deep blue eyes. Her name was Lynette McNichols-Bodine. She was twenty-six and the mother of four-year old Trevor Bodine. The child inherited black hair from the paternal side of his lineage, but he possessed his mother's deep blue eyes.

Trevor and his mom were released from the hospital the same evening with a clean bill of health. The other Jack was admitted. Sheriff Jack went through the girl's handbag for information about her. Turned out her name was Jacklynn McNichols. Neither her drivers license nor her student ID, from Ohio State, showed a middle initial. It appeared the girl was a twenty two-year-old grad student. He cataloged the contents of the bag: a wallet, seventy-eight dollars, a checkbook, one credit card, and birth control pills. Her one piece of luggage, retrieved before the HP impounded her car, contained several changes of clothes and a couple of veterinary textbooks. No makeup, not even a tube of lipstick. No wants or warrants.

He sure had his hands full trying to keep her quiet at the truck stop. "Don't Move" he'd warned her. "You hit your head when you fell. An ambulance is on the way." From the way she fell his concern had been head or spinal injuries. At that point, he'd noticed blood seeping through her down-lined vest. Carefully, he'd unzipped it to discover the inside of the nylon vest along with the sweater beneath it was soaked. He'd looked over at Henry, but somehow controlled the urge to put a bullet between his eyes too; the brute had managed to cut her before Carter could subdue him. Jack took a clean towel, supplied by a quick thinking waitress, and applied pressure to the wound while they waited for help to arrive. He had decided to delay questioning the girl after she was treated at the hospital. The paramedics stabilized her neck before treating her wound. She was sliced from just below her left breast to her hip. Her injuries would have been much worse had it not been for her thick vest.

Jack woke the following morning around five, gulped a cup of black coffee, and headed back to the office to relieve Carter. The other three deputies were out on patrol. As usual, Carter brought him up to speed on the overnight and early morning activities.

"The girls' parents arrived at the airport just before three this morning. They, along with Lynn and Trevor, are up at the hospital. Henry Bodine has lawyered up. He is claiming that the woman shot him, locked him in the outhouse, and abducted his nephew and his brother's wife. Part of his story is that she parked the tractor on his truck and then shot the tires out on both. She also stole Bobby's guns, loaded them in his truck, and drove it off the bridge into the river." Carter chuckled and shook his head. "I sure hope she pulls through. I would love to hear her side of the story."

Jack nodded in agreement. He also hoped little Jack made it. "Go get something to eat, Carter. Then head home. I've got it from here." Jack decided to see what he could dig up on the Bodine brothers.

Chapter Four
A New Dawn

April 30, 2011

Jack nearly jumped out of his skin! The phone had come to life with a vengeance. His heart was racing double time; he took a deep breath and willed it to slow down He was getting too old for all this drama. He must have dozed off over his desk, and the landline almost split his eardrum. Most of the calls were from family and friends searching for storm victims.

He was about to give his wife's cell another try, but his desk phone rang again. All the tension drained out of his body when he answered and heard her voice. His first question was, "Are you and Lisa okay?"

"We're fine. Our grandson made an early entrance, so Lisa and I drove to Tampa to get a look at our boy, John, and Millie's new son. How are you? We heard the county got hit pretty hard."

"Extensive damage. We lost some folks, and some are still unaccounted for. A lot of people are homeless, including us."

"But how are you, Jack?"

"I'm fine, now that I've heard from you."

"Sorry, love, but we couldn't get through. Lisa was told not to return to school and that graduation would be postponed until at least August. Tuscaloosa is for all purposes gone, and the university is being used to shelter survivors."

"Well, I guess you got your wish; I'll put in for retirement after some normalcy has returned."

"We'll be home in a few days, once the roads are opened."

Jack glanced out the window and took in the dawn.

"It looks like it's going to be a beautiful Alabama sunrise. See yah soon, little Jack."

Not Nearly The End...

Find out what lead Jack McNichols to the truck stop confrontation with the Bodine brothers. She ends up under arrest and on trial for kidnapping. Look for "Jack's Alabama Sunrise" coming soon.

A SNEAK PREVIEW:

Backyard Horse Tales 3.

DON'T CALL ME LOVE
by
Jackie Anton

Love's adventures are only beginning. Look for the complete accounting of this unpredictable spotted wonder's memoirs to be released in print complete with illustrations.

Illustrator:
Sandy Shipley

Scheduled print release is the fall of 2015.

Chapter One
Lazy Summer Days

I became a backyard horse my yearling summer. Until that fateful summer I lived on a large horse farm not far from where I was to spend most of my life. My mother was the boss mare, and she told me while I was still a little filly nursing at her side, "Never let any of the other foals push you around. Timid horses don't fare as well as the more aggressive ones."

Momma was always the first in line to enter the barn for the evening feed, and no one challenged her. As I became more aware of the hierarchy of herd life I grew a little bolder, straying a little farther from my mother's side. Under the guidance of my mother, her traits soon became mine. I heard whispers around the pasture that I did not understand. I took my curiosity to Mom, "What does *Plain Jane* mean?"

"Where did you hear that, daughter?"

"The other foals said their moms call you and Toy *Plain Janes.*"

"It is just sour apples! Little ones only repeat what their parents say, and some of the other mares are jealous. Toy and I don't have Appaloosa coat patterns, but we both produce loud colored foals. Don't pay any attention to them."

"Well, I think you're the most beautiful of all the mares, Mom."

She nuzzled me. "Thank you dear, you're a lovely filly, and you will be a real beauty."

I didn't know about that, but I did have some spots the color of my mom's solid coat. She told me once that the color was called "liver chestnut." I'd inherited the same star mom had in the middle of her forehead, but my star was not as easily seen amid the spots that covered my face. No matter how hard I stared at my reflection in the pond, or the water trough I could barely see it. My hind socks were also inherited from Mom, and they stood out well on my dark chestnut legs. From my knees and hocks up my body was white with multi-colored spots in various sizes some even had what Mom called a halo around them.

Toy was Mom's best friend. She'd been injured as a young horse, and the mishap left her blind in one eye. Mom, like a good friend, always stood on Toy's blind side to protect her. Toy was buckskin, which is kind of a gold color with a black mane and tail. Her legs were black from her knees and hocks down. She also had a few random white spots on her gold coat, her spots were about the size of a kernel of corn. Her daughter, Sugar, was born a couple of days after me, and we palled around together a lot. Sugar was the name the humans gave to Toy's foal. My new friend was a true leopard, white from her nose to her hooves. She had large, quarter and half-dollar size, golden spots splashed about on her white coat. In the same way that some of my spots and the color of my legs matched my mom's coat, Sugar's spots were the color of Toy's golden coat.

Sugar thought that we were related because I had a few gold spots here and there in my coat too, along with some reddish chestnut spots. Actually Sugar was pretty close with her relationship estimate. As our mothers explained the facts of life to us, it turns out we were half sisters. Now the word from the older generation was that every one of our sire's offspring had at least one red chestnut spot somewhere on their body. Some of the foals, like me, had several spots of that color on their hides. It became a game with us to locate the inherited spot on the other foals.

"Hey Sugar the only red spot that I see is on the back of your right ear." I told her, after a close inspection of her coat pattern.
Some of the famous marks were well hidden, and could get you kicked if you got too personal in your search.

"Watch out for Bertha and her friends." Sugar warned me. "They are a nasty bunch. It's a lot safer to check out the colts."

We tired of the game after a few days of attempting to catalog the hereditary spot on the rest of our pasture mates. The new topic of conversation was the strange humans who came to gawk at us.

" Sugar, do you find it strange that the people tramping

through our pasture, and peeking into our stalls call us both leopards?"

Sugar thought about my observation before offering her viewpoint. "Even though your dark legs keep you from being a true leopard, according to our mothers, you look enough like one to fool people."

"That's just silly, Sugar. Mom told me that leopards are white from head to hoof with spots on their coats. She said some have a lot of Appaloosa markings and others practically none at all."

The human population of the farm, as well as visitors, started calling me Love. Like all foals, I sought my mom to explain what I didn't understand. "Mom, what does Love mean?"

"Well, daughter, I overheard one of the grooms tell another that you were registered as Chelsea Love. So, the humans gave you Love as your barn name."

I had no idea what registered meant, but I filed it away in my memory banks. What I did know, was that I took a lot of teasing once word of my name got circulated to the other horses. The harassment about my name continued throughout the fall, and winter. I guess that the other mothers thought I was misnamed. The constant teasing did not do my disposition any good. Fall arrived, and we were all put in a separate pasture from our mothers. I kicked and bit a few of the other weanlings butts when they repeated what their had mothers had told them.

Sugar went away with some unfamiliar humans a few days before Christmas. We didn't even get to say goodbye! The colts were separated from us fillies in the spring. We had all grown a lot throughout the long year. I could see Mom with her new foal over in the adjoining pasture. My new sibling didn't look at all like me! The new foal had a big snowflake pattern on its rump, but otherwise was solid like our Mom, with the same star and hind socks. "Oh, my! Mom's new foal is a colt." I snorted. Toy had lost her foal a couple of months earlier, so my little brother had two overprotective mares keeping him in line to make sure he didn't get too adventurous too soon. He couldn't get away with anything.

No one much bothered me anymore, they knew better, but the little filly Blue was always picked on, and excluded from the filly clique. I guess that when Sugar and I were growing up together we didn't pay much attention to the other foals, except to put an occasional upstart in their place. I never realized how small Blue was.

Blue, alone as usual, had found a yummy patch of clover not far from where I was grazing. The gang of four—the nasty girls that always made fun of my name—decided they wanted Blue's patch of clover.

"Scram, midget, you don't rate sweet clover."

Outnumbered, Blue started to back off. When she saw me coming at her from behind she must have felt trapped. She halted her retreat and froze in her tracks not sure how to escape. Bertha, the ringleader of the pack, was so occupied bullying Blue that she didn't notice me. She laid back her ears and scrunched up her nostrils making an ugly face at Blue, and then threatened her. "I told you to get lost, Blue, unless you want a beating!"

I whizzed past the frightened Blue, and took a chunk out of big mouth Bertha's spotted hide. Then, I whipped around and clocked her with a hind foot for good measure. One of her friends, Lotta, tried a rear attack. I let go with both hind legs and sent her flying off of her feet. The other two members of the gang were long gone. I laid my ears back and challenged them, "Come on! You want to try again? I'm just getting warmed up." They backed off, and I turned my attention to Blue.

I'd never noticed before—probably because she tried to stay out of everyone's way—but Blue was very pretty with her black coat and white snowflakes. I told her, "Eat your clover, Blue, they won't be back."

"Thank you Love! Would you share the patch of sweet clover with me? I am sure there is enough for two."

After that day, Blue became my new pasture buddy. A few weeks later the gang of four became the gang of three. By the end of the month the humans call *June*, they became the gang of two. It was funny...or maybe not...but as their numbers dwindled so did their bullying.

Another four weeks passed and a family of humans took Blue with them. I left the farm of my birth a few days after my new little friend. I wondered if I would ever see my mother and little brother again, or my friends Sugar and Blue.

I was very reluctant to leave everyone that I knew, and all that was familiar to me. But my new humans were persistent, and spent a lot of time with me. From the beginning it required all their patience to convince me to step into the metal box on wheels. From the safety of my pasture, I'd watched other horses go into the trailer trap, and they all disappeared never to be seen again. I didn't know where they went, but I didn't want to disappear like the others. If I held my ground, I thought they might give up and go away.

Chapter Two
New Herd, New Rules

The short ride to my new home was frightening. They had tricked me with a bucked of the yummy sweet feed that I loved. Then they sprinkled some on the floor of the scary trap. My hunger for the molasses-coated grain defeated my resolve. As I reached farther into the trailer to nibble at the oats and pellets, I made the mistake of hopping in to reach more of the tasty offering. The metal stall on wheels shook and wiggled when my hooves hit the rubber-covered floor. Then wham! The doors closed behind me with a loud noise that echoed around the metal trap. That scared the poop right out of me! I forgot all about the grain that I was busy grinding under my scrambling hooves.

The whole experience would have been a lot more traumatic if the human named Terrie hadn't ridden in the trailer with me on that first fateful trip. She understood that I was terrified when the stall began to move. "Oh. Great Horse in heaven please save me!" I prayed. My human companion reassured me by stroking my neck and talking to me in a soft voice, *"Easy, Love, you will find your balance soon, we are almost home."*

I was not really adept at the human language yet. But I thought I had just left my home behind, along with my mom and little brother. I took the measure of this young woman: her hair was a lighter shade of gold than what Toy's coat had been, and she had eyes the color of the summer sky. She looked kind of skinny to me, but it was hard for me to judge. I did not know many humans.

My companion was right the bumpy ride was soon over. The stall stopped moving, and the door behind me opened once more. Terrie pushed on my chest while telling me to *"back up."* Okay, time out! I didn't have a clue what she was yakking about. She repeated the words, and poked me in the chest again. I took a step back, and she stopped jabbing at my chest to praise me. *"Good girl, Love."* So, cautiously, I took a couple of more steps back, and suddenly my back foot slipped out into midair. I quickly brought it back in with my other feet. It took me a couple of false starts, and a lot of work on Terrie's part to get me out of that thing. Once I got <u>both</u> hind feet back on solid ground my front end was out of there in a flash. I thanked the great horse gods for getting me out of the frightening ride in one piece. Toy had always told Sugar and me that if we were good fillies, the great horse in heaven would look out for us. My mom just used to snort at her friend's comment. I don't know if Mom didn't believe in the horse spirits, or she figured that I couldn't be good long enough to qualify for divine protection.

To be continued ......

ABOUT THE AUTHOR

Jackie Anton is an accomplished equestrian with a lifetime of experience: as trainer, exhibitor, 4-H and youth club coach, as well as a horse show judge, the author brings many years of working with horses and young riders to her award winning Backyard Horse Tales Series.

Uncharted Storms is a collection of short stories aimed at Young Adult and older readers. Look for more short tales in the future.

Backyard Horse Tales: Sox 2nd Edition brings to light the mutual love between a handicapped colt and a lonely child with a learning disability. Find out how this pair team up to triumph over life's roadblocks, and why their story won the prestigious Mom's Choice

Award of Excellence for Family Friendly Media. (Reading level age 8 through Adult)

BYHT 2 "Frosty and the Nightstalker" was one of four finalists in the E-Book Fiction category for the Next Generation Indie Book Awards. Then the paperback went on to earn the Mom's Choice Award for Juvenile Historical Fiction.

Jackie is hard at work on BYHT 3 Don't Call Me Love. You can catch a peek at Love's beautiful cover on the Backyard Horse Tales Face Book Fan Page:
http://www.facebook.com/pages/Backyard-Horse-Tales/190283981002767

The author is a mother of two grown children and grandmother of two. She and her husband of forty-three years continue to ride daily. They live on a mini-farm in rural Ohio and share their little slice of horse heaven with two Quarter Horses, a Haflinger, a rescued dog, and a calico barn cat.

If you enjoyed "Uncharted Storms: Short Stories of Hearts at Risk," please take time to review it.

AUTHOR NOTES:

I hope you enjoyed the collection of tales and characters in "Uncharted Storms" as much as I enjoyed creating them. "A Tumble in the Snow" was the first encounter Annie has with Mack. Their story continues in the novel "Mac's Blue Eyed Mistress." Watch for the release date on my writing blog http://jackieanton.com/ and my author website.

Please take a few moments to review this book on Amazon, Smashwords.com, Barnesandnoble.com, and any other review sites that you have access to. Reader's feedback helps me know if I got it right.

I love to hear from my readers and fans. Contact me at *talesbyjackie@gmail.com* and while you are there let me know if you would like to be added to my quarterly newsletter.

Thanks for choosing this book. Happy reading!

Online Autographs for e-books:
http://www.authorgraph.com/authors/backyardhorse

Author's Website:
http://talesbyjackie.com

AUTHOR INTERVIEW:

AN INTERVIEW WITH AUTHOR JACKIE ANTON

Question: Would you share with our followers the inspiration behind your latest book release?

Jackie: Uncharted Storms: Short Stories of Hearts at Risk was the result of all the speculation with the approach of the 2012 New Year and the end of the Mayan Calendar. I have been on this earth long enough to have experienced several of these world ending predictions.

There are people who take these things to heart and children are most susceptible to the constant bombardment by today's media of such hysterics.

The idea took hold to write a story of a young person caught up in the hype and the concept for the first tale in Uncharted Storms was born. I borrowed my granddaughter's first name for the young heroine in "Terra Beyond 2012."

Question: Is this a genre you usually write in?

Jackie: This collection of stories is my first attempt at offering a work to the Young Adult reader. Adults are also enjoying the e-book released in 2014 prior to this print version. Thus early reader reviews mention only five tales when there are six in this book.

Question: Do you have other published works?

Jackie: I also have two illustrated chapter books for readers age eight and above. Horsemen and animal lovers of all ages have embraced "Backyard Horse Tales." The third book in the series in in the works and should be released soon.

Question: Jackie do you have a pseudonym?

Jackie: Yes, my Adult novels are penned as J. M. Anton

Question: Jackie have you won any recognitions or awards that you would like to share?

Jackie: At the time of this printing "Backyard Horse Tales: Sox 2nd Edition" sports the Mom's Choice Awards Seal of Excellence on its cover. The second book in the BYHT Series "Frosty and the Night Stalker" is accumulating multiple awards as an e-book and paperback. Frosty went to the 2013 BEA as part of the Next Generation Indie Book Awards as one of four finalists in the E-book General Fiction category. On his way home from New York he was honored with the MCA Seal of Excellence in Juvenile Historical Fiction. I think there may be another award or two in 2015 for this Appaloosa's tale.

Question: Do you have an agent or a publicist? If your collaboration is positive, feel free to give them a little plug.

Jackie: Carol Upton was my publicist for two years and was a joy to work with. An animal lover and horse enthusiast, Carol embraced Backyard Horse Tales. She published reviews and excerpts in horse publications, arranged interviews for me, and introduced me to some awesome fellow authors. Carol lost her battle with cancer in 2014 and will be missed by myself and many other authors who became her friends as well as her clients.

Question: Are your books available in print, e-book, or both?

Jackie: Beginning with my second book the e-book versions are released prior the print versions. That allows me to assess readers' responses.

Question: Illustrations or photos for covers are so important to successful marketing. Do you use an illustrator or photographer for your book(s)?

Jackie: Both photos and illustrations have been used in the production of my books. Sox my first Backyard Horse Tale was illustrated by me. The photo on the cover was taken by my daughter, Kellie, who also did the cover work for one of my adult novels. The covers and interior illustrations for BYHT 2 & 3 are the work of illustrator Sandy Shipley.

Question: How much of the marketing do you do for your book(s), and for yourself as a brand?

Jackie: I haven't found a replacement for Carol who relieved me of the stress involved with much of the online promotion and allowed me to spend more time writing. I guess the ball is in my court on that front again. Most of my success and book sales come from special events and book signings where I am able to interact with readers. I am always looking for more ways to spread the word. Discount sales to book clubs is another productive avenue.

Question: Do you spend much time in research, or do you write from experience?

Jackie: The best way to answer this question is to declare that I do both. My experience with horses and youth have lent authenticity to my Backyard Horse Tales. Sox didn't take much research, but Frosty's tale required a lot of time to research the historical data.

Many of the aspects of Uncharted Storms including the title required some research.

Question: What Point of view do you feel most comfortable with, first person or third?

Jackie: First person and the horse's point of view are used for the Backyard Horse Tale Series. It takes a bit of thought to work in the human element when the horse is telling the story. However, the majority of my books are written in the third person.

Question: Jackie, what is your view on e-books?

Jackie: I have to admit that it took me a while to get a handle on the e-book issue as an author. On the positive side readers and students don't have to lug around stacks of books when they travel or commute to classes. My grandchildren have iPad readers and are able to take reading material with them anywhere in the world. Fortunately, they still enjoy printed books too.

I still like the feel of a book in my hand and can flip the pages back to check on a fact in a previous chapter with much more ease that can be accomplished on my Kindle.

This interview was part of the blog tour, June 4ᵗʰ of 2014, for "Uncharted Storms" e-book. It has been updated to include this book.